"I am Zhigani of Mios," the old ⌐ louder and more authoritative than it had been before. Even with just one eye, her icy blue gaze locked on Driskoll and Kellach and held them fast.

Kellach and Driskoll blinked, waiting for her to explain.

"This means nothing to you?" she asked.

The brothers exchanged a glance. She seemed upset, and they didn't want to make matters worse.

"Are you a friend of Zendric's?" asked Kellach.

"Zendric." She repeated the name slowly, frowning. "Yes. Where is he?"

"Oh, he's in—oof!" Driskoll glared at his brother for elbowing him.

"Oof?" She frowned. "I know no Oof. How do I get to this Oof?"

"We don't know where Zendric is, exactly," said Kellach. "But we'll give him a message next time we see him, if you'd like."

Zhigani dismissed the idea with a wave. "Forgive me. There has been some mistake. Behold!"

She raised the black orb before them. "The Eye of Fortune sees what lies in store for you!"

EYE OF FORTUNE

DENISE R. GRAHAM

KNIGHTS
OF THE
SILVER
DRAGON

BOOK 4

COVER & INTERIOR ART
EMILY FIEGENSCHUH

MIRROR
STONE

Eye of Fortune

©2004 Wizards of the Coast, Inc.

Distributed in the United States by Holtzbrinck Publishing. Distributed in Canada by Fenn Ltd.

Distributed to the hobby, toy, and comic trade in the United States and Canada by regional distributors.

Distributed worldwide by Wizards of the Coast, Inc. and regional distributors.

Art by Emily Fiegenschuh
Cartography by Dennis Kauth
First Printing: December 2004
Library of Congress Catalog Card Number: 2004106850

9 8 7 6 5 4 3 2 1

US ISBN: 0-7869-3169-8
UK ISBN: 0-7869-3170-1
620-96537-001-EN

U.S., CANADA,
ASIA, PACIFIC, & LATIN AMERICA
Wizards of the Coast, Inc.
P.O. Box 707
Renton, WA 98057-0707
+1-800-324-6496

EUROPEAN HEADQUARTERS
Wizards of the Coast, Belgium
T Hofveld 6d
1702 Groot-Bijgaarden
Belgium
+322 457 3350

Visit our website at **www.mirrorstonebooks.com**

For Ron

~

for all the days filled with magic
and adventure
and laughs

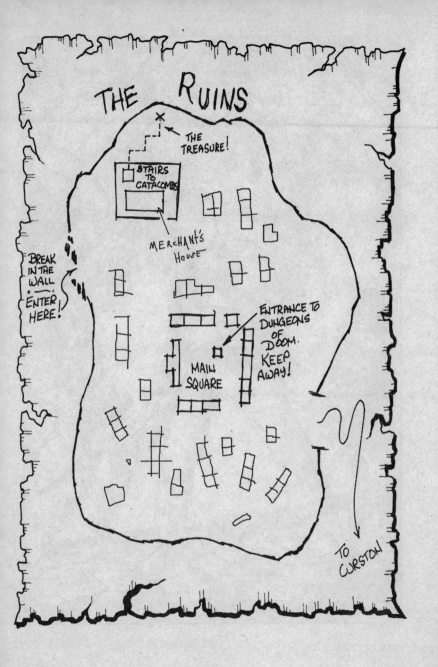

CHAPTER

1

G ive it up, Driskoll," Kellach said. "Just because a wandering minstrel showed you a spell doesn't mean you can do it too."

The minstrel's wagon lurched over a rut in the road, and a bag of costumes fell on Driskoll.

Driskoll shoved away the bag and shot his brother a dirty look.

"I did it once."

"Keep it down, you two," said Moyra from the back of the dark, stuffy wagon. "If the minstrel finds out we stowed away back here, he'll dump us in the middle of the road. Do you want to ride to ValSages or walk all the way back to Curston?"

A few days earlier, a man had visited Curston, spreading tales of the celebrated City of Vices, as ValSages was fondly called. The lure of an entire city devoted to fun and entertainment had been more than the three kids could resist. They'd made up excuses to tell their parents and Zendric and smuggled themselves onto the minstrel's wagon for a day of adventure in the big city.

To pass the time on the way there, Driskoll was trying to cast a spell the minstrel had taught him. He'd done it once with the minstrel's help, but so far he hadn't been able to repeat it.

"Making a statue say 'proon frabble' doesn't count," Kellach whispered. "You cast the spell to make it say 'shoo, pigeons!' but all you got was gibberish."

"I know I can do it. Just watch." Driskoll took another scrap of wool from his jacket pocket.

Just then the wagon rolled to a halt. Kellach peeked through a knothole in the door. "We're here! As soon as we're out of sight of the guards here, we'll jump out. Get ready!"

After a brief, breathless pause, he hissed, "Now!" He opened the door and hopped out onto the road, followed quickly by Moyra and Driskoll. They shut the door as the wagon rolled away.

As Driskoll's eyes adjusted to the bright sunlight, the city's wonders overwhelmed him. ValSages sparkled as if someone had planted a gemstone and a magical city of jewels had sprung up from it. Delicate spires reached toward the heavens. Sculptures, waterfalls, and arches surrounded massive domes of silver and gold.

The streets of ValSages overflowed with entertainers and visitors of all races. The shouts of vendors hawking their wares clashed with an endless array of music and the never-ending clink of coins.

"Souvenirs!" shouted a halfling from atop a handcart laden with cheesy trinkets. Painted tankards, strings of beads, and other gaudy mementos all bore the names of various game halls.

"Get your souvenirs here! The Oasis! The Inner Sanctum! The Swashbuckler! Only in ValSages! Collect them all!"

"The Swashbuckler!" said Moyra. "I heard they have a free show there with pirate ships battling across the glass ceilings. Let's go!"

The Knights headed down the main thoroughfare toward the Galleria, which held several of the best game halls. Driskoll gazed around in awe, trying to take in everything at once.

A knife whistled past Driskoll's ear, snapping him out of his daze. He had wandered into a circle of warriors juggling razor-sharp blades of all shapes and sizes. Driskoll froze as daggers and scimitars danced in deadly arcs all around him.

A crowd gathered around.

"Look at that fool!" a man shouted.

"He's no fool," one of the warriors boomed. "He just knows of our amazing skill. Right, boy?"

"Um, whatever you say," said Driskoll, eyes wide. He kept very still.

The blades clanked to rest in the performers' hands.

The warrior laughed. "It's so nice to be appreciated."

Moyra dragged Driskoll from the circle. "Okay, guys, time for a few rules. First, pay attention!" She gave Driskoll a look.

"Next," she said, "try to stay clear of the big crowds and keep a good grip on your coins. This place is crawling with pickpockets and scam artists."

She eyed the Silver Dragon pin on Driskoll's pack. "And you might want to hide that, so it doesn't get stolen."

"I put it there to warn off cutpurses," he replied.

3

"Oh, please," said Kellach. "You put it there to show off."

"Did not," Driskoll said.

"Come on, you two!" Moyra dragged them into the current of people moving along the road. "You're wasting time. Let's go see the pirate show."

"Did you see the way those warriors threw those blades?" said Driskoll, hurrying to keep up with her. "I'm going to learn to do that!"

"Let me know when you decide to start practicing," she said.

"You want to practice together?"

"No, I just want to make sure I'm on the other side of town when you do."

"Oh, ha-ha." He gave her a playful shove.

Ahead, a broad stairway swept up to a gilded arch. The tide of tourists carried the three friends up the stairs into the grand entrance hall of the Galleria, an indoor city with shops, eateries, and game halls under soaring ceilings of glass.

Just past the main entrance, Moyra caught sight of a tall post completely covered in arrow-shaped signs. Each sign pointed in a different direction. She found the one that read "The Swash-buckler" and grabbed Driskoll's and Kellach's arms. "This way!" she said.

They wound their way along the path, past a quartet of satyrs dancing, an asp swaying to its charmer's flute, and a sword swallower.

Around the first bend, in front of a shop selling cloud candy, Moyra spotted a game of skill she just had to try. It required crawling across a rope bridge that flipped easily

4

from side to side. She mastered the tricky apparatus on her first try.

The man in the booth handed her a small bag. She reached in and pulled out a few large metal jacks with pointed ends. "Excellent! These ought to come in handy some day."

"What are those?" asked Driskoll.

"They're caltrops," said Kellach. "You toss them in the path of someone you want to slow down. They're made to land point-up."

"Ouch," said Driskoll, looking at the wicked little spikes.

"Exactly." Moyra dropped them back into the bag and tucked it into her belt.

Across the way, Driskoll noticed a bookshop. Near its wide entryway stood an old woman holding a sign that read "Fortunes told. Palms read."

"Hey, look!" he said. "There's a fortune-teller. Let's go see what she says."

Moyra gave him a nudge. "Come on, Driskoll. She's bound to be a phony. You don't honestly think you're going to find a real clairvoyant in the game halls of ValSages, do you?"

"Well, no." Driskoll couldn't keep the disappointment from his voice. "I just think it'd be fun."

Kellach smiled. "Ah, come on, Moyra. Only in ValSages . . . " he said, quoting the city's slogan.

"Oh, all right," she said, shaking her head. "But let me go first. I'll show you what a phony she is."

They wound their way through the crowd toward the whip-thin woman in faded silks. She seemed to be scanning the crowds, hardly noticing their approach.

As Driskoll stepped up behind her, she held out her hand without turning around. "One silver."

Driskoll hesitated. "Me? How did you know. . . ?"

"Here you go." Moyra dropped a coin into the crone's pale hand.

The old woman's stiff fingers curled closed. When they opened again, the coin was gone. She turned to face Moyra. "Your palm."

Moyra rested her open hand in the fortune-teller's and grinned. She kept peeking at the boys and trying not to laugh.

"Ah, a skeptic," the old woman said without looking up. She traced the lines on Moyra's palm with her fingertip. "I see hardships, some overcome, some yet to come."

Moyra scoffed. "That's true of everyone."

The fortune-teller went on. "Your Skill line is quite strong. Your Energy line shows the power of youth extending farther than usual. See here? The line of Will fades in places, but the Charm line joins it here. The area between them is the Domain of Chance, and it reveals great opportunities that come with great risk."

Moyra flashed her friends a smug grin. "See? A little flattery and some general mumbo jumbo. That's all it is." She tried to withdraw her hand.

The old woman held it fast. "I see a grand palace in your future. This mark reveals that you will be late yet right on time. This area below it marks the Domain of Souls. This tells us that quite soon, you will find nothing is as it seems, and sticks and stones change everything."

"Right. Me in a palace. What a bunch of hooey!" said Moyra. "I'm not paying for this! I want a refund."

"I foresaw that you would," said the gypsy, nodding toward Moyra's open hand. The silver coin lay nestled in her palm.

"Oh, you did not," Moyra countered, withdrawing her hand. She turned to the brothers. "You guys can waste your silvers if you want. I'm dying of thirst. I'm going to get some dragon's draft at that cafe up ahead."

The brothers watched her jostle her way through the crowds.

The old woman gave a small shrug and held out her palm. "One silver."

"Mm," Driskoll agreed. He reached into his pack for a coin.

As he did, the crone's eyes widened. With astonishing strength she grabbed his wrist. "Where did you get that?" she demanded.

He followed her gaze to his pin, and his chest puffed up a bit. "Our friend Zendric gave it to me. We all got them," with a nod he indicated Kellach and Moyra's retreating form, "when we became Knights of the Silver Dragon."

"Knights? Children? This can't be . . . " The gypsy released Driskoll and covered her face with her hand. Her shoulders sank, and she muttered under her breath.

"Are you all right?" Driskoll asked.

The fortune-teller's hand came away with a damp popping sound. There, cradled in her palm, was her left eye. It wasn't a real eye nor even an ordinary glass eye. It appeared to be some kind of black crystal.

Driskoll fell back a step. He tried not to stare at the woman's empty eye socket, but he couldn't help it.

7

"I am Zhigani of Mios," the old woman announced, her voice louder and more authoritative than it had been before. Even with just one eye, her icy blue gaze locked on Driskoll and Kellach and held them fast.

Kellach and Driskoll blinked, waiting for her to explain.

"This means nothing to you?" she asked.

The brothers exchanged a glance. She seemed upset, and they didn't want to make matters worse.

"Are you a friend of Zendric's?" asked Kellach.

"Zendric." She repeated the name slowly, frowning. "Yes. Where is he?"

"Oh, he's in—oof!" Driskoll glared at his brother for elbowing him.

"Oof?" She frowned. "I know no Oof. How do I get to this Oof?"

"We don't know where Zendric is, exactly," said Kellach. "But we'll give him a message next time we see him, if you'd like."

Zhigani dismissed the idea with a wave. "Forgive me. There has been some mistake. Behold!"

She raised the black orb before them. "The Eye of Fortune sees what lies in store for you!"

CHAPTER

2

The crystal flashed silver, then turned clear. A hazy image appeared within it and slowly solidified. It was a treasure chest. Carved into its open lock were two dragons snarling at each other. From inside the chest spilled jewelry, gems, and coins.

"A treasure!" Driskoll exclaimed. "For us? Where is it? How do we find it?"

The image flickered and faded. In its place, another began to take shape.

A face formed, slowly coming into focus. It was a girl with black hair pulled into a high ponytail. Her sculpted features looked vaguely elven, and she looked angry.

The fortune-teller gasped.

"Who's that?" asked Driskoll.

"I don't know," Kellach answered, thinking his brother was asking him. He rubbed his chin and peered at the face in the crystal, waiting for more information.

Zhigani shook her head. "If you don't know her, she is of no importance."

The crystal went black.

The old woman slipped the Eye back into place, and it looked exactly like her other eye. "The Eye reveals many things, but we cannot truly know their meaning until their moment is upon us. Such is the way of Fortune." She gazed thoughtfully at them. Then she added, "But you won't find it standing around here. You must go."

A young couple approached and the gypsy turned to them, palm out. "One silver," she said.

Driskoll and Kellach exchanged curious glances as they rejoined the human current flowing along the cobbled path.

"Well, that was quite an impressive performance," said Kellach at last.

"What was?" asked Moyra, coming from the opposite direction. She held a cup out to Driskoll. "Want some dragon's draft?"

"I've always wanted to try this. Thanks." He took a sip from the cup and began to cough.

Tears streamed down his face. "Good stuff," he wheezed, handing the cup back to Moyra.

"What was so impressive?" she repeated.

Kellach told her about Zhigani's eye and what it had shown them, while Driskoll recovered from his coughing fit brought on by the spicy dragon's draft.

"The Eye had to be some kind of trick," said Moyra.

"If it was," said Kellach, "it was a really good one."

They walked on, and at last the path opened into a broad plaza revealing the entrance to the Swashbuckler Game Hall. Its towering facade was shaped like an enormous treasure chest overflowing with gems, gold coins, and bejeweled weapons.

As they headed across the plaza toward the entrance, shouts rang out from the crowds inside the Swashbuckler. People fled in all directions as a hideous two-headed creature emerged from the game hall.

Thirteen feet tall, it towered over tourists and locals alike. Both of its faces had a piggish snout and yellow teeth, and it wielded heavy clubs in both hands. The fake parrot between its two heads and "Only in ValSages" eye patches marked it as an agent of the Swashbuckler Game Hall.

As it snarled and stormed out into the plaza, Driskoll's legs suddenly felt like quicksand beneath him.

"Escaped slave!" shouted one of the monstrous heads.

"Return for reward!" growled the other.

"An ettin!" said Kellach. "Someone must have cast some serious spells to make it fit for that job. Normally its stench alone would make it useless around civilized people."

The three friends moved out of the creature's way. Moyra scanned the plaza, as if the slave might be standing around, waiting for her to catch him and collect the reward.

"Coming through!" snarled the right head.

"Coming through!" snarled the left head.

The ettin stopped in its tracks. "I said that already, Pains, you stupid," said the right head.

"Don't call me stupid, Aches!" The left arm brought its club down on the right head with a loud *bonk!*

"Ow! Cut it out!" The right arm brought its club down on the left head with a great *thud!*

"Shut up, both of you, and get back to work!" squawked the

fake parrot, though its beak did not move. Clearly someone was talking through it from somewhere else. The two heads glared at the parrot.

Bonk! Thud! Feathers flew from the crumpled remains of the fake bird.

"Oh, you guys are going to get it when you get back here," squawked the flattened parrot. "Now go find that slave!"

Aches and Pains exchanged guilty looks, then slowly lowered their clubs. "Yes, Master," the heads mumbled together. The creature stumbled out of the plaza and down the path, the crowds scrambling to get out of its way.

"I'm getting a bad feeling about this place," Driskoll said. "I heard the game hall slaves are all criminals working off their sentences. The one that escaped could be a murderer!"

Moyra shook her head. "The slaves are mostly either cheaters or people who couldn't pay their gambling debts. Think about it. The game halls wouldn't want slaves killing off their customers. Besides, no matter where we go, there'll be plenty of criminals that haven't been caught."

"If you're trying to make me feel better, you're doing a really lousy job of it," Driskoll said, only half joking.

They went into the Swashbuckler. Inside its dazzling entrance stood a sign stating that the Fantastic Pirate Presentation had just ended. The next one wouldn't start for another two hours.

"Why don't we go over to the Inner Sanctum, then?" Kellach suggested. "I hear they have a mermaid show and an enchanted fountain that sings and dances."

"Won't we have to walk halfway across the Galleria to get there?" asked Driskoll.

"You have anything better to do?"

Driskoll happily admitted he did not. "Inner Sanctum Game Hall, here we come!"

On the way back, Moyra ducked into the cafe for a refill of dragon's draft. As she raised her souvenir cup to take a drink, a girl in a gauzy costume pushed past her, bumping her arm.

The dragon's draft splashed all over Moyra's face and clothes.

"Hey!" Moyra yelled, glaring after the girl.

The girl didn't even look back. She cut through the milling crowds at a dead run, leaving a wide gap in her wake.

Up ahead, the kids saw Zhigani reach out and grab the girl's arm. The girl's black ponytail whipped around as she spun, giving the three friends a good view of her scowling face. Her high cheekbones and gracefully arched eyebrows suggested a trace of elven ancestry.

"That's her!" said Driskoll. "The girl from the crystal eye! Maybe she knows something about our treasure."

Moyra rolled her eyes. "Can't you see? She's working with the fortune-teller. I knew that old lady was a phony."

The gypsy leaned close to whisper in the girl's ear. The girl shook her arm loose from the old woman's grasp, and the filmy sleeve of her costume revealed part of a scar on her forearm. The old woman held up her cupped hands. Light filtered through her ancient fingers. The girl's eyes widened.

"Let's just find out what she knows," Driskoll said. "Hey!" he called out. "You with the ponytail!"

The girl spun toward him. She had the most amazing eyes, like blue ice.

At that moment, several entertainers wearing a giant silk dragon costume danced across the path, cutting off Driskoll's view of the girl.

By the time the dragon passed, the girl had vanished.

Driskoll gaped at Kellach and Moyra. "Where'd she go?"

Moyra shrugged. "She probably ran off with the fortune-teller."

Driskoll looked again. Moyra was right. Zhigani was gone too.

"Let's get going," said Kellach, "so we can get back in time for the next Pirate Presentation."

They resumed their trek to the Inner Sanctum. On the way, at a crossing of two main passageways, Driskoll spied a fire breather and joined the circle of spectators surrounding her.

The woman placed a slender torch in front of her lips and blew. Flames burst forth, curling into the shape of a snarling gargoyle before flaring into tongues, then sparks, then smoke.

He continued to watch as she presented one fantastic creature after another. When her performance drew to a close, Driskoll reluctantly turned to his friends.

Only they weren't there.

"Kellach?" Driskoll called out. "Moyra?" He turned in a slow circle, scanning the crowd as it drifted apart. Moyra's red hair usually made her pretty easy to spot.

"Kellach? Moyra? Very funny, you guys! You can come out now." This drew some odd looks from passersby.

He had to force himself not to break into a run. Don't panic, he thought. Just because you're all alone in an enormous city full of criminals is no reason to panic. Kellach and

Moyra would never leave you. They've got to be right around here somewhere.

But where?

First he scoured the passageway between the fire breather's area and the Swashbuckler.

No sign of them there.

Then he scanned the large crossway.

Still no sign of them.

One by one, he checked what he could see of the narrow side paths that branched off from the larger passageways. The Galleria's many side paths ran at odd angles and had so many twists, a map of the place would look like a plate full of snakes.

It was near the corner of one of these side paths that he spotted her.

Not Moyra, but the girl from the crystal eye. There she was, stealing a tunic from an overturned cart! Her high black ponytail whipped around as she glanced over her shoulder.

Driskoll couldn't resist. He hurried up behind her and, in a low but clear voice, said, "I think we should talk."

She glared down at him. "Stay away from me!"

The girl pulled the tunic on over her costume. She was almost as tall as Kellach, and her arms under her gauzy sleeves were long and sinewy.

"But the fortune-teller—" he began.

Before he could say another word, a large shadow fell over them.

"Well, look who's here," a voice rumbled.

CHAPTER

3

Driskoll and the girl instinctively took a step back from the huge half-orc looming over them. The edge of the cart against their backs halted their retreat.

The broad, tusked face pressed in close to Driskoll's. The half-orc's breath smelled of old meat. "Surprised to see me, runt?"

Of all the rotten luck, Driskoll thought. Miles from home in a city full of strangers, and he ends up toe to toe with Kruncher's old sidekick, Thrash.

"Um, I'm a little surprised," Driskoll managed at last.

"You shouldn't be," the larger boy said. "I told you I'd get you and your puny friends for what happened to Kruncher. I promised I'd make you pay." A quick shove emphasized this last point.

The girl stood as if she'd been turned to stone.

"What do you say I buy us a round of dragon's draft," Driskoll said. "And we talk this whole thing out. You know, give me a chance to explain what really happened."

The half-orc glanced casually from side to side. "I don't see your daddy around here anywhere, runt." His eyes narrowed, and a hideous grin split his face. "Does Daddy even know you're here?"

Driskoll swallowed hard. "He—um—"

"Ha! This is perfect!" The half-orc's fist hauled back. "I'm going to beat you to a pulp, and when you get back to Curston, you won't be able to turn me in, because you'd have to tell your daddy where you were!"

Just as Thrash prepared to strike, a tiny man in a hooded cape stepped in front of Driskoll. "Did I hear someone say Curston?"

"Who the blazes are you?" Thrash demanded.

"Shh! You want everyone to hear?" The little man peered furtively in all directions. From a pouch he pulled a tattered, rolled up parchment. "There is a chest full of treasure hidden in the ruins near Curston, and this map leads right to it. I'll sell you this map, but you mustn't let it fall into the wrong hands."

Driskoll glanced at the girl and the half-orc, and he knew they had found something they could all agree on. This man was crazy.

The man must have read their expressions, because he began talking very fast. "Now, I know what you're thinking," he said in hushed tones. "You're thinking, why would anyone sell a treasure map instead of using it to find the treasure themselves? Well, the truth is, I can't go after the treasure, because there are some very bad people after me.

"It's all just a big misunderstanding, mind you. But don't bother trying to explain that to them!" He started pacing and

17

waving his arms. "No, indeed. And after all I did for them!"

Suddenly he seemed to notice Driskoll and the other two again, catching their puzzled expressions. With an apologetic look, he held up one hand.

"But I digress. The important thing is, I need to get as far from here as I can. So my misfortune becomes your good fortune. The three of you can work together. Split the cost of the map, the risks, and the treasure. What do you say?" He beamed at them.

The half-orc jerked his thumb at Driskoll and the girl. "I say I don't need any help from a useless runt and some bit of fluff."

"Bit of fluff?" The girl leveled a cold gaze at Thrash. It was the first time she'd spoken since he arrived. "Ever had your nose bloodied by a bit of fluff, tough guy?"

This brought a bark of laughter from the bully. "Come on, Fluffy! I dare you. Give it your best shot. You only get one, though, so you'd better make it good."

With both fists raised over her head, she lunged at him.

He caught her wrists easily and laughed in her face. "Anyone ever tell you that you fight like a girl, Fluffy?"

"Break it up, you two," said the man in the cape. "You'll bring the guardsmen—"

But Fluffy's foot was already a blur of motion. Back, up, above her shoulder. *Whap!*

The half-orc roared in pain, and both his hands went to his face.

"Ah! What the—?" As Thrash's palms came away from his face, Driskoll could see blood streaming from his nose.

Driskoll's jaw dropped. He turned to congratulate the girl,

but she was already slipping away toward the main passageway. The man in the cape had made himself scarce too.

Driskoll didn't want to be the only one standing around when Thrash recovered. He turned and headed after the girl.

A pull on his arm swung him back around. Meaty paws clamped onto the front of his shirt, lifting his feet off the ground.

"Where do you think you're going, runt?" the half-orc bellowed into his face.

"Uh, I was just—"

"To the nearest healer! That's where you're going." Thrash shook Driskoll, rattling his teeth. "Because you're going to take the beating for your little friend!"

"She's not my friend!" Driskoll stammered between shakes. "I don't even know her! Hurry! You can still catch her!"

The shaking stopped. "Which way did she go?"

"That way!" Driskoll pointed down the side path, in the opposite direction from where he'd last seen the girl.

Thrash dropped Driskoll and scanned the crowds.

Driskoll's bones jarred as his feet hit the ground. With the half-orc distracted, he reached into his pocket for a scrap of wool. Singing a tune under his breath, he focused his concentration on an area just down the path. Then he waited, ready to run.

From several strides ahead of Thrash came a voice that sounded like the girl's. The spell had worked!

Well, sort of. The effect Driskoll was after was the girl's voice calling, "Look out! Coming through!" and so on. But the words didn't come out exactly the way he'd planned.

"Proon frabble!" the girl's voice cried.

The half-orc turned to glare at Driskoll. "Did she say 'Proon frabble'?"

"Dve piver blurbfsp!" the spell-voice shouted. "Jigwump!"

"It's Fluffy!" Driskoll said. "She's loony. And you're letting her get away!"

"Bleekinpflax!" The voice called from a bit farther down the path.

Thrash hesitated, then gave Driskoll a shove. "I'll pay you a visit in Curston, runt," he called over his shoulder as he raced off into the crowds.

The man in the cape stepped out from behind the cart and smiled at his remaining customer. "Bleekinpflax?"

"Only in ValSages," Driskoll replied. He tried to laugh. But a squeak came out instead.

"Look," said the man. "I can see you're a good kid, and I'm running out of time. So I'll cut you a break on the map. How much have you got on you?"

Driskoll edged toward the main passageway. "Um, I really should be going. Maybe the guardsmen can help you . . . "

"No!" The man grabbed his arm and pulled him close. "It's not safe. Some of them have been bribed. I— arrh!"

The man gasped and clutched his neck. His hand came away holding a throwing dart painted with black-and-red snakes. He stared at it in horror. "It's too late for me now," he rasped. "These snakes are the mark of my enemies. I'm poisoned."

The man fell against Driskoll's shoulder. The map appeared in the man's hand once more, and he pushed it at the boy.

Driskoll's hand closed reflexively around it. "But—"

"Take it!" the man whispered fiercely. "And take your friends with you! Put the treasure to good use. My enemies would only use it for evil."

"But—"

"Run, boy!" the man wheezed, propelling him back toward the main hallway. "Run, or you'll be next!"

And with that, the man collapsed facedown on the ground.

CHAPTER

4

Driskoll ran.

His breath came in ragged bursts. Up the main passage he fled, past gnome illusionist shows and dwarf comedy troupes, through costumed partygoers and caravans of traders. At last he reached the broad, marble staircase of the Inner Sanctum.

The shallow steps curved up and around a pool. At the center of the pool, streams of water surged into the air and converged in the shape of an orchestra. Though the musicians were made of mist, the music they produced was real. Around them danced a circle of mermaids.

As Driskoll started the long climb to the glass- and gold-encased entryway, he heard voices shouting his name.

"Driskoll! Up here!"

At the top of the stairs, he spotted Kellach and Moyra waving from atop a statue of a pegasus. He waved back and ran to meet them.

When he got there, Moyra had already jumped down. She

held out a hand to Kellach for balance as he slid down and landed beside her.

"Where did you go?" they all demanded at once.

"I turned around and you were both gone!" said Driskoll.

"We walked straight over here from the Swashbuckler," Moyra countered. She pointed down to the fountain. "We've seen those mermaids do that same water ballet four times already. One minute you were there, and the next minute you weren't. We were about to notify the guardsmen."

Driskoll felt the color drain from his face. "You didn't talk to any guardsmen, did you?"

"Of course not. You know they're never around when you need them. See? Here they come now, because we don't need them anymore." She gestured toward the steps. Two guardsmen were descending the stairs, both munching on puffs of spun sugar. "Ooh, that cloud candy looks good," said Moyra.

"We have to go!" Driskoll said in a harsh whisper. "We need to get out of town! Now!"

"What?" said Kellach. "Why?"

"Don't make eye contact with the guards, and don't say anything," said Driskoll. "Just follow me!"

∎ ∎ ∎ ∎ ∎

An hour later, tucked safely inside a merchant's cart bound for Curston, Driskoll told Kellach and Moyra all that had happened.

"So what do you think?" he asked.

Kellach squirmed in their cramped, stuffy niche. He was taller than the younger two, and it was harder for him to squeeze into these hiding places. "I think if this crate of cheese doesn't quit jabbing me in the back, I'll dump it overboard," he grumbled.

Moyra frowned. "I can't help wondering, why you? Out of all the people in ValSages, why did the man choose you, a half-orc thug, and that weird 'Fluffy' girl to try to sell the map to? Are you sure the whole thing wasn't just a show put on by one of the game halls?"

"Yes, I'm sure," Driskoll insisted. "We were nowhere near any of the big game halls, and no one paid any attention to us. If a game hall went to the trouble to put on such an elaborate show, wouldn't they want an audience?"

Moyra shrugged. "Then it was probably just another scam. None of them picked your pockets, did they?"

"No," said Driskoll.

Kellach wedged his pack behind his back, still trying to get comfortable. "You have to admit, since the man is dead, his enemies seem to have been pretty real."

"That's why he gave me this map." Driskoll pulled the rumpled parchment from his jacket pocket. "He said his enemies would only use it for evil."

Moyra shook her head. "It's got to be a fake."

"Probably," Kellach agreed.

The three of them jounced along in silence for a few moments.

"But—" said Kellach. A playful gleam lit his eyes as he exchanged a knowing look with his brother.

"It could be real," Driskoll finished the thought.

"We ought to at least investigate," said Kellach.

"Besides," Driskoll added, his expression growing serious,

"that map may lead to important information about the man's murder. I feel guilty leaving him lying there like that. I should have told the guardsmen."

"But he himself said it wasn't safe," Moyra said. "He told you to take the map and run. You granted his dying wish."

"Thanks," he said. "But I'll feel better if I can grant the rest of it and keep the treasure from his enemies. When you look at it that way, I have a duty to go look for it."

Moyra held out her hand. "Let's see that map again."

Driskoll passed her the battered scrap of parchment.

She unrolled it against the side of a barrel, where they could all see it. The map showed the ruins outside Curston. A notation in the northwest corner indicated the former residence of a wealthy merchant. A maze of catacombs sprawled beneath it. It was there that the alleged treasure was hidden.

"You do realize this map leads down to the Dungeons of Doom," Moyra said.

Driskoll nodded.

"And you still want to go?"

Driskoll nodded again.

"Well, I still think it's bogus." She crossed her arms. "Count me out."

"Oh, come on, Moyra," said Kellach. "We'll need you down there. We'll just go far enough to see if the map even matches the terrain. Then we can decide whether to walk away, keep going, or get more help. Think about it. If this treasure turns out to be real, you want a share. Right?"

With a little more persuading, Moyra reluctantly agreed to go along. The three of them arranged to meet at dawn just beyond the walls of Curston, where the clearing ended and the trees began. From there they would sneak off together into the ruins once more.

CHAPTER

5

The next day, Driskoll and Kellach sat waiting on a downed aspen near the road and just inside the tree line. Their gazes turned again and again toward Curston's Westgate.

They had gathered as many supplies as they could comfortably carry. Since they had no idea what to expect on this journey, they tried to bring a little of everything. At the same time, they tried to pack light. They didn't want to be bogged down if they needed to make a quick escape, and they definitely wanted to have plenty of space and energy left for carrying treasure.

"No Silver Dragon pin today, Dris?" Kellach asked.

"I left it at home, so it doesn't get lost or anything," his brother replied. "It's not like I *always* wear it."

The older boy grinned. "You would if people wouldn't make fun of you."

"Oh, go kiss a troll."

Kellach stood, squinting into the rising sun to take one last look toward the gate. "I guess Moyra decided not to come after all."

"Do you think we should wait a while longer? Maybe she just had trouble sneaking out of the house." The idea of just the two of them venturing into the ruins made Driskoll nervous. There was more than enough danger for three skulking among the rotting remains of the old city. The place was crawling with goblins, wild animals, the undead, and no telling what else.

"Trouble sneaking out? Moyra?" Kellach scoffed. "Not likely. You know she didn't really want to come." As if reading Driskoll's thoughts, Kellach added, "Look, we won't go very far today. We'll just check it out—see if the path this map shows even exists."

Driskoll stood up and peered at the gate. Still no sign of her. "All right. Let's get going then. If Dad catches us out after curfew, we'll be safer with the monsters."

They trekked along the main road to the path that branched north from it, leading to the ruins. The map indicated a break in the wall of the ruins a short way north of its westernmost point. The boys had never been to that part of the old city. They decided they had a better chance of getting to the merchant's residence without running into any goblins or the like if they skirted the ruins by way of the surrounding forest. So when they reached a point just south of the ruins, they veered off the old road to circle west, then north again.

The trees here huddled close together. The woods fell silent as the boys trudged through them, the birds and animals suspicious of the intruders. In spite of the bright, clear day, little sun penetrated the gloom under the leafy canopy. Driskoll imagined dozens of pairs of eyes watching them. He felt tempted to whistle a tune to lighten the mood but knew that would only draw attention to them, maybe the attention of someone or something not satisfied to just watch. His hand went instinctively to the hilt of his sword, even as his other hand swatted at a bug on his back.

An explosion of noise and a blur of movement to their left made both boys jump. Without thinking, Driskoll drew his blade and hurled it end over end at the source of the commotion.

A rabbit zigged and zagged through the undergrowth, its white tail waving them a farewell as it disappeared into the distance. Driskoll's sword thudded against the moist earth, never getting anywhere near its target.

"Driskoll!" Kellach exclaimed. "Are you crazy?"

Driskoll ran his fingers through his hair. "Sorry. Guess I've got a *hare* trigger. Get it?" He forced an awkward laugh, trying to cover his embarrassment.

"Watching one blade juggling act in ValSages doesn't make you an expert." His brother rolled his eyes and shook his head. "I've never seen you so twitchy."

"I said I was sorry," he grumbled, retrieving his sword and sliding it back into his belt. "I keep thinking that man's enemies will come after me."

"Well, if they're out here, they certainly know where we are now," said Kellach, giving his brother a stern look.

"I know. I'll be more careful," Driskoll promised.

They walked on. At last they found what they were looking for, a crumbling gap in the ancient city wall. Two grown men could walk through it side by side. Several large, gray blocks that had toppled to the ground now lay scattered on either side of the wall. Weeds grew among the debris.

"Here's the break in the wall, just like the map shows," said Kellach, heading for the gap.

Driskoll stopped him with a hand on his shoulder and pointed.

From beneath one gray block jutted a skeletal hand. The arm bones poked out of a hollow in the earth underneath the block. It looked like some kind of den.

"Do you think something's living under there?" Driskoll asked, keeping his voice low.

"I don't know," said Kellach, "but let's not find out. Come on." He stepped around the block and through the gap in the wall.

Driskoll didn't move. "Maybe we should turn back."

His brother regarded him evenly. "I thought you wanted to look for this treasure. It is *your* map, after all."

"I do want to look for the treasure."

"Then why are you stalling?"

Driskoll scuffed his boot in the dirt. "It's just . . . I don't know. What if they're waiting for me?"

"Who? The man's enemies?"

Driskoll nodded.

His brother sighed. "Driskoll, if they knew where to wait for you, they wouldn't need the map. Right?"

The younger brother thought about that. "Oh, yeah. I guess you're right."

"So actually, the safest thing for you to do is to follow the map, because they don't know the way. And if they had planned to take your map, don't you think they'd have made some sort of move by now? Maybe around the time you threw your sword away?"

Driskoll gave him a sheepish grin. "Seems reasonable when you put it that way," he said.

"I'm so flattered you think so," Kellach said. "Now can we please get going?"

Driskoll stepped through the gap. Whatever buildings had once stood here had been scoured to almost nothing by the passage of time. Slightly clearer areas suggested streets and alleyways between the rubble of what might have been houses or shops. The boys passed quickly through this quarter, keeping their eyes peeled for any goblins.

The destruction of everything else in the area made the next leg of their journey so obvious, they could have managed it without the map. They made their way to another wall, this one lower than the ancient city's outer wall, though slightly better preserved. Iron reinforcements were all that remained of what must have been heavy wooden gates.

The boys walked cautiously toward the empty gateway. Beyond it stretched the overgrown courtyard of a once-proud estate. The palatial home lay in tatters. Scorch marks covered much of the remaining walls of the three-story carcass. Its empty windows gaped like dead eyes. The entire west wing had collapsed upon itself so long ago that a blanket of plants had grown over its broken stones.

Utter stillness ruled this place. The catacombs below had long fostered tales of undead hordes, so many adventurers avoided this spot. The site looked deserted.

The two brothers hurried up the wide path and swung around the east wing to the back of the residence, keeping a safe distance between themselves and the eerie building.

From the brambles rose a still-stately mausoleum, ghostly white against the grays and greens of stone and vegetation.

The map indicated this was the entrance to the catacombs.

Though the marble walls had somehow withstood the passage of ages, the door had disintegrated entirely. The boys stepped slowly, almost reverently, over the threshold.

Outside, the day was warm and sunny, but inside the vault, all was cool and hushed and dim. The light through the open doorway reflected from the alabaster floor, illuminating sleek columns and smooth walls in an awe-inspiring glow. Only a vacant pedestal in the corner to their left kept watch over the stairway to the catacombs below.

Driskoll checked the map again. "This must be it," he murmured.

"Well, little brother, so far it looks like your map is the real deal." Kellach took his lantern out of his pack and lit it.

Together, they began the long descent.

CHAPTER

6

At the bottom of the stairs lay the catacombs, twisted, seeping tunnels filled with the dead of ages. Bones and plundered caskets lay strewn among the cobwebs and dust. Centipedes scuttled away from the lantern light.

With Driskoll giving directions from the map, the brothers ventured deep into the musty vaults, their steps echoing off the low ceiling. As they stooped through a sagging archway, Driskoll noticed an unpleasant detail. The area appeared to have been undisturbed for centuries, except for a very fresh trail of footprints through the dust. He stopped and glanced over his shoulder.

"Don't tell me we took a wrong turn," said Kellach.

"No," his little brother replied. He hesitated, then added, "But I feel like we're being followed."

Kellach shined the lantern back up the path. They waited, muscles tense, ears straining to pick up the telltale rattle of gear in a pack or the scrape of a claw.

After several long moments, Kellach lowered the light. "I

don't hear anything. I think you're just being paranoid again."

The younger boy let out a sigh. "I hope you're right."

In a remote chamber, they found the entrance promised by the map: a hidden door within an empty casket standing against a wall. The boys moved into the corridor beyond it. Up ahead about twenty feet, the path took a sharp left turn.

The wall facing them bore strange carvings of intertwining shapes, some resembling animals, others vines. The boys crept closer, squinting at the designs, trying to make sense of them.

And then they were falling.

With a thunderous crash, a trapdoor in the floor had dropped out from under their feet, sending them plunging into blackness. The lantern flew from Kellach's hand and smashed somewhere below, making the darkness complete.

They fell just a few feet before they hit the bottom with sharp yelps of pain. Only it wasn't the bottom. It was a smooth, almost vertical incline, which sent them shooting even deeper into the trap, their wails trailing behind them.

Driskoll's hands flew out blindly as he sped down the chute, but he found no handholds, nothing to slow his descent.

Suddenly, even the incline was gone, and Driskoll and Kellach were free falling. They took the only logical course of action available in such circumstances.

They screamed.

"AAAHHH! . . . ," yelled Driskoll.

"AAAHHH! . . . ," yelled Kellach.

". . . OW!" they yelled together.

The free fall had only lasted another ten feet or so. They had finally hit bottom.

34

Driskoll groaned and tried to sit up.

"Are you all right?" Kellach asked from somewhere quite near in the darkness. His voice sounded strained.

"I think so," Driskoll replied. "Something cushioned my fall a little."

"Yeah, that was me." The older boy gave him a shove. "Would you mind getting off now?"

"Oh, I'm sorry! Are you okay, Kellach?" A rattling sound emerged from beneath them as Driskoll moved aside.

"Just bruises, but—"

"I should have known!" a deep voice snarled beside them.

The boys jumped.

"Who's there?" asked Driskoll, his voice quavering.

"Don't play innocent with me, runt," the voice said. "I still owe you a beating anyway."

Another deep voice joined in. "Who is that, Thrash?"

"Quiet, Lunk," the half-orc replied before turning his attention back to the brothers. "You twerps made a big mistake, following me like this."

"If we'd been following you," said Kellach, "we'd have avoided this trap."

"Ugh!" said Driskoll before Thrash could answer. "What is that stench? It smells like death itself crawled in here to die."

From the blackness, a disembodied voice hissed, "It did."

CHAPTER

7

All the boys, human and half-orc alike, let out startled cries.

A light flared, filling the pit.

They all fell back, shielding their eyes. Thrash leaped to his feet, fists ready.

Driskoll squinted against the sudden brightness. His hand closed around the hilt of his sword, but he stayed seated. If Thrash wanted to have first crack at whatever it was, that was fine with him.

The light tightened into a beam aimed at their feet. Within the beam lay a body, facedown, a red stain in the middle of its cloak.

The beam widened, and they saw they had landed on a huge pile of bones in a round pit. The bones filled the lower part of the pit, obscuring the bottom somewhere below. Propped against the curved wall was a rotting corpse, the source of the stench.

As the boys' eyes adjusted to the light, a form began to take shape behind it. Humanoid, slender, a high ponytail—

"Fluffy!" Thrash exclaimed. He started toward her with a menacing grin.

The light narrowed to a brilliant ray blazing into the half-orc's face. He fell back, throwing his arms up to protect his eyes.

The strange light was coming from a small orb in the girl's hand. Driskoll had never seen any lantern like it. It had to be magical.

"The fortune-teller's Eye!" said Kellach.

Knotted around the Eye and hanging from the girl's neck was a string of beads, cheap souvenirs from ValSages. The beads allowed the girl to wear the orb like a necklace.

"Pretty," said the half-orc called Lunk. Even seated, Lunk was massive. Thrash seemed frail compared to him. Lunk scooted closer to the girl and stretched one finger toward the necklace.

"Careful," she said gently. "Big magic."

The big half-orc withdrew his finger and stuck it in his mouth. His gaze flicked from the orb to the girl and back.

"How did you get the fortune-teller's Eye?" Driskoll's eyes narrowed at the girl.

"Maybe I stole it," she snapped back. "Maybe she gave it to me."

"Have you been sitting there listening to us this whole time?" Thrash shouted. "What's the matter? Afraid to fight when you can't run away?"

"I remember you," Kellach interrupted, drawing Thrash's attention away from the girl. "Weren't you a relative of Kruncher's or something?"

At the mention of Kruncher's name, Lunk growled. His expression held something more than just anger, however. Something that looked like pain.

"He was my cousin." Thrash eyed the brothers suspiciously. "And if you twerps weren't following us, what are you doing here?"

Driskoll raised an eyebrow at Kellach.

Kellach shrugged. "You might as well tell him. It doesn't look like this place was such a big secret to begin with. And if any of us get out of here, it'll be even less of one."

Driskoll looked around and picked up the map from where it had landed. Holding it up for Thrash to see, he said, "You know that guy in ValSages, the one who wanted to sell us that map?"

"You mean that guy?" the girl asked. She shined the light on the dead man in the middle of the pit, lighting up his face.

Driskoll's jaw dropped. "It's him!" he exclaimed. "But that's impossible. He's . . . dead!"

"Really?" Thrash said sarcastically. "How long did it take you to figure that one out, runt?"

"No, I mean he was dead before! Back in ValSages." Driskoll briefly described what happened after the others left him alone with the man in the cape.

"But if this guy died in ValSages, how'd he get down here?" said Kellach. "Maybe he can tell us." He rolled the dead man over and began searching his pockets and packs. In one, he found several rolled up pieces of parchment. He drew one open.

"It's a map." He held it up for the others to examine.

Driskoll frowned. "That looks just like the one he gave

39

me." He held his map up next to it to compare them. They were identical.

The two boys opened one parchment after another. All they found were more copies of the same map.

"He must have been running some kind of scam, like Moyra said. What else was he carrying?" Kellach tossed the last map aside and pulled a pouch off the man's belt. "Maybe—"

"Hey!" Thrash grabbed the pouch out of Kellach's hand. "If there's any loot on him, it's mine."

"Well, that seems fair," said Kellach.

His sarcasm was lost on the bully. Thrash took out a dart from the pouch.

Driskoll frowned. "That's the poisoned dart he pulled from his neck."

Kellach inspected the man's neck. "I don't see any puncture mark, but it might just be too small. Can I take a look at that, Thrash?"

The bigger boy hesitated, then he tossed the dart over. "I wouldn't waste my time with such a puny weapon anyway."

Kellach picked it up and glanced at it. He placed the tip against the pit wall and pushed. The point collapsed harmlessly into the body of the weapon.

"It's a fake," he announced. "A trick." He passed it to his brother.

Worked into its black-and-red snake design were the words "Only in ValSages."

Driskoll rolled his eyes. "I can't believe I fell for that. I've seen stage weapons just like it, usually daggers or swords, but basically the same thing. He must have been carrying it all along, planning to fake his death. I guess I could understand it if he actually got people to pay him, but why go to all that trouble to *give* away phony maps?"

The others contemplated this in silence. Thrash pocketed the few coins he found, then slid the man's dagger from its leather sheath. He started to slip it under his own belt, paused, put the tip against the side of the sheath, and pushed.

The blade pressed a small dent into the leather. Satisfied, Thrash added the weapon to his already impressive collection.

Meanwhile, Kellach pulled a crumpled scrap of paper out of another pocket. "Look at this. It's another map. A different one."

"Maybe it's the real treasure map!" Driskoll leaned over to look at it. "What's it show?"

"None of your business, runt," the half-orc grunted, shoving the smaller boy away and grabbing the map. He wadded up the paper and stuffed it in his own pocket. "This map's all mine."

Driskoll let out an exasperated gasp. With a shake of his head, Kellach warned him not to argue. Driskoll sat back and crossed his arms.

Kellach continued his search. From the next pocket, he produced a piece of paper, folded and sealed with red wax. "Looks like some kind of note," he said, tearing it open and scanning its contents.

"'Fugitive still missing,'" he read aloud. "'Allies located. Luring into pit for questioning and elimination.'"

"Elimination!" cried Driskoll, shocked out of his anger. "He was planning to kill us? Why? I don't know anything about any fugitives or allies. Do you?" He looked to the others, who shook their heads. "What does any of this have to do with us?"

"What do you mean 'us,' runt?" Thrash said in a dangerous tone. "You're the one who had the map."

"Yes, I've been wondering about that," said Kellach. "If you guys didn't have a map, how did you end up here?"

"We followed her." With a nod, the half-orc indicated the girl. Four curious gazes turned toward the girl.

She shrugged.

"Once I got you off my trail," she said to Thrash, "I doubled back to go get a map. He must've expected one or both of us would fall for it, because the man was still waiting there after this one left." Here she motioned toward Driskoll. "And he was still very much alive."

"So he wanted you dead, too," said Thrash. Slowly he rose to his feet. "What do you know about all this?"

"Nothing. I—" The girl started to get up. "Ouch!" She sat back down hard.

Lunk had been sitting peacefully the entire time. Now he reached out with his finger again. "Ouch," he said, pointing at the girl's ankle.

It was red and badly swollen. His finger moved closer.

"Don't!" said Driskoll. "You'll hurt her."

"He's all right," said the girl. "I listened to these two long enough before you got here. Just watch."

Carefully, Lunk touched his fingertip to the injured area. A noise that sounded like a cross between a growl and a sneeze tumbled from his lips. A violet glow appeared around the girl's ankle, then quickly expanded, turning a deep indigo. The half-orc removed his finger, and the glow winked out of sight.

The girl's ankle no longer showed any sign of injury.

Around her neck, the light from the fortune-teller's Eye suddenly dimmed, then flared again. It happened so fast, the boys might have thought they imagined it, except that at the same time, the girl let out a startled gasp.

"I saw . . . I saw . . . "

"What?" asked Kellach, quickly looking around for signs of danger. "Is everything all right?"

"Yes," she said. "I didn't see it with my eyes. An image just flashed through my mind, like a vision. I'm not sure what it was. It was like this"—she held up the orb—"only different." Her face clouded, and she shook her head as if to clear it.

"I'm sure it was nothing," she said tersely.

She jumped to her feet, shifting her weight, first tentatively, then with more confidence, onto the injured ankle. "Look! I'm good as new," she said, giving Lunk a pat on the head. "Thanks, big fellah."

He unfolded to his full height and patted her on the head in return. "Nice, good Fluffy," he said with a lopsided grin.

"My name is Calyssa," she said, pointing at herself for emphasis.

"Fluffy," he said, pointing at her, his grin even bigger.

She shook her head. "Ca-lyss-a," she repeated, pronouncing it slowly for him.

"Fluffy!" the big healer replied. He seemed to think it was some kind of game.

"Lunk," said Thrash, adjusting his weapons, "quit messing around and give me a lift out of this hole. These losers can stay down here and play fugitives and allies till they rot."

Driskoll looked to Kellach, who shook his head. Thrash's plan would never work. The pit was too deep, and the walls were rounded at the top to keep anyone from getting a decent grip on the ledge.

Lunk patted "Fluffy" on the head in farewell. Hands clasped together, he leaned over to give Thrash a boost.

Thrash placed his boot in Lunk's hands. He hopped up, tried to get his other foot onto Lunk's shoulder, lost his balance, and toppled to the bone pile with a clatter. As he struggled to sit up, he glared at the others, daring them to make fun of him. He gave it two more tries before giving up.

"Too bad we didn't bring Locky," said Driskoll. "He could fly back and bring help."

Thrash glowered at Driskoll. "You got us all into this, runt. I ought to pick you up and throw you up there, but you're too scrawny to pull me out."

"Fortunately," said Kellach, "Driskoll and I don't have to rely on brute strength." He removed a bit of string and a piece of wood from his spell component pouch and held them out in front of him. With his free hand, he traced an intricate design in the air.

Driskoll thought Kellach was laying it on a bit thick, but he couldn't decide whether he was showing off to impress the half-orcs or the girl. At the same time, he had to admire his brother's ability to cast spells. His own first attempt at magic hadn't turned out as gloriously as he'd imagined.

"Hey!" said Thrash, grabbing Kellach by the collar. "Nobody's going anywhere without Lunk and me."

"You said yourself we're too small to pull you out," said

44

Kellach. "But if you give us the real treasure map, we'll send a party back for you."

"Yeah, right," said Thrash, his voice growing louder.

"Hey, we're not street thugs like you!" Kellach snapped back. "Our word is good!"

"Back it down, you guys," said Driskoll. "You can fight later. Right now we have to work together, or we'll all rot down here. Thrash, let Kellach and me go, you keep my pack for ransom, and we'll send someone back for you."

"He can go," Thrash countered, "and I'll hold you for ransom."

"No way!"

"It's all right, Dris," said Kellach. His older brother gave him a sly look that said he had a trick up his sleeve. "I can handle it."

Giving both brothers a threatening look, the half-orc turned the older one loose.

With a flourish, the apprentice finished casting his spell.

Nothing happened.

Kellach frowned. "I don't understand. This makes no sense at all."

"Something wrong?" asked Thrash.

A deep blush crept into Kellach's cheeks. "The spell failed."

The half-orc burst out laughing.

"I've cast that spell dozens of times."

Thrash laughed even harder.

"Probably the interruption ruined it," Kellach seethed. "Go ahead. Laugh it up. That spell was going to get us all out of here."

Calyssa had been watching all this without comment. Now she moved closer to Lunk. "Hey, big fellah. I think you dropped something." She pointed to a coin behind his feet.

Driskoll was sure it hadn't been there a moment ago.

When Lunk turned and bent to pick it up, Calyssa went into action.

She ran up Lunk's broad back, sprang off Thrash's shoulder, and leaped out of the pit.

The glow from the Eye receded.

Calyssa was gone.

CHAPTER

8

Fluffy!" yelled Thrash, as Driskoll hauled a torch from his pack. "I'll get you for this!"

A sudden light from above spilled down on them. "Just for that, I should leave you down there," said the girl, peering at them over the edge of the pit. "I was just looking for a place to tie off a rope before saving your ungrateful hide."

"Hey, I'm still down here, Fluffy."

"And quit calling me Fluffy. My name is Calyssa. Now throw me a rope, you big lout."

Thrash grumbled and folded his arms. "I don't have a rope," he muttered.

"What?" said Calyssa. "How could you not have a rope?"

"How could *you* not have a rope?" he retorted.

She held out her arms, palms up. "I'm not the one who needs one."

He scowled up at her. "When we started following you, we didn't know we'd be getting into anything like this."

"Then what's all that in your packs?" asked Kellach.

"A few more weapons," said Thrash. "But mostly it's food for Lunk."

"Food?" said Lunk, his face brightening.

"Oh, great," said Thrash. "See what you started?" He had Lunk turn around while he rooted through his pack. He pulled out a hunk of meat and handed it to Lunk. The big healer devoured it in what must have been record time.

While all this was going on, Driskoll uncoiled a rope from his pack strap. He hesitated, then tied one end around his waist.

Fluffy, or Calyssa, or whoever the girl was, didn't seem the type to take his rope and leave them all to die, but the man in the cape hadn't seemed the type to kill him, either.

He tossed the other end of the rope up to Calyssa. It took a couple of tries, but at last she caught it.

Driskoll and Kellach went up first, with Thrash and Lunk helping from below. It would take the combined strength of the smaller three to pull up one of the half-orcs.

Driskoll expected Thrash to insist on going first, but Thrash surprised him, linking his fingers together to help Lunk up. He wondered why the bully acted so differently with his simple-minded sidekick, but he didn't have the nerve to ask.

Once they had all reached the top, they took stock of their situation.

A ten-foot-wide ledge circled the pit. The opening they had fallen through was in the ceiling another ten feet above them, with a steep slide leading from it into the pit. Three sturdy wooden doors with iron reinforcements ringed the ledge, spaced evenly apart in the surrounding stone wall. Strange, elaborate carvings, much like the ones they'd seen right before falling into the pit trap, covered the doors and the walls between them.

Kellach looked at the hole in the ceiling, then at the three doors. "Which do you think is the easiest way out of here?"

"Out of here?" said Driskoll. "I don't know. I thought we might look around first. I mean, we came all this way."

"Yeah, and it almost got us killed," Kellach replied.

"But that's exactly the point," Calyssa chimed in. "Someone out there wants him— I mean us—dead. I don't know what this is all about, but I don't think any of us will be safe anywhere until we get some answers."

"She has a point," Driskoll said. "Maybe our trouble ended with the death of that con man down there, but then again, maybe not. We need to find out. Even if we get a chance to go back to ValSages, we have no leads to go on there. We should see what we can find out down here."

The three of them cast questioning glances at Thrash.

"Don't look at me," he said. "You're on your own. Lunk and I are out of here. I only ended up down here because I wanted to get back at Fluffy. But since she didn't leave us in that pit when she could have, we'll call it even."

Lunk pulled a knife from his belt and held the hilt out to the girl.

"No, Lunk," said Thrash. "You can't give her your good knife."

Lunk stuck out his bottom lip. "I give a present to nice, good Fluffy."

Thrash gave a growl of exasperation. "Oh, all right. We'll give her this one."

He handed her the dead man's dagger. "Here. Now you owe me."

A smile played about Calyssa's lips. "Thanks, I think." She slipped the weapon into her belt.

Thrash turned to face Driskoll and Kellach. "You two still have a beating coming, but I'm going to let it slide for today."

"If you're leaving," Driskoll said, "why don't you give us that other map we found?"

Thrash shot him a wicked grin. "Because we'll need it when we come back with friends and supplies."

"Just out of curiosity, how do you plan to get out of here?" asked Kellach, peering up at the almost vertical slope leading to the hole in the ceiling. "I don't think even Calyssa can get back up that way. Or can you?"

She shook her head. "Not a chance."

"Okay," said Driskoll. "Then right now it doesn't matter who's going or staying. Either way we need to see what's behind those doors. So why don't we work together? Whatever we happen to find, we can decide what we want to do from there."

"We don't need you twerps slowing us down," said Thrash.

"Hey, big fellah," Calyssa said to Lunk. "You want to work with us for a while. Right?"

Lunk beamed. "We stay with Fluffy."

Thrash glared at the girl. "All right, Lunk. But only till we find a way out of here."

This seemed to satisfy everyone. They turned their attention to the three doors. The word "PULL" was inscribed on each of them in several languages, including common and orc, from top to bottom.

"The doors all look the same," said Calyssa. "Which one should we try first?"

"They're not exactly the same," Kellach replied. "That handle only has one notch in it." He pointed to the door to the right of the slide.

"That handle has two," he added, pointing to the door opposite the slide. "And that one has three," he said, pointing to the door on the slide's left.

"I say we start with that one first," said Thrash, pointing to the door with one notch in the handle. The others shrugged.

Kellach grasped the handle of door number one. "Everybody ready?" he asked.

No one answered, and their silence spoke volumes. Thrash drew a greataxe from its holster at his back. Lunk raised a heavy mace. Calyssa held her new dagger, testing its weight in her hand. Driskoll reached for the hilt of his short sword, but kept it sheathed. He was better at talking his way out of trouble than fighting, and a blade in his hand wouldn't help him gain anyone's trust. He nodded to his brother.

Kellach pulled the handle.

The door didn't budge.

He pulled again, this time harder. Nothing happened.

Thrash gave Kellach a look of pure contempt. "Let me do it." He lowered his weapon, grabbed the handle and pulled.

Nothing.

Thrash frowned at the door in disbelief. He leaned his greataxe against the wall, grasped the door handle with both hands and hauled on it. His thick muscles strained with the effort.

51

Still nothing. He turned to the others.

"Push," Lunk said.

Driskoll tried not to laugh.

Kellach gestured toward the door and the word "PULL" so plainly covering it. "Oh, right. Push! Why didn't I think of that?"

"He can't read," Thrash explained.

At the same time, Lunk apparently mistook Kellach's gesture as an invitation to try the door. Resting his mace on his shoulder, he stepped up and pushed against the door.

The door swung wide without so much as a squeak.

For a moment, everyone but Lunk stood blinking, completely dumbfounded, at the open door and the empty passageway beyond.

Calyssa was the first to shake it off. "I'm sure there's a very logical explanation for this. But right now I just don't want to know what it is."

The five of them started down the stone corridor.

A short way into the passage, Driskoll stopped and turned. "Did you hear that?" he whispered.

"What?" asked Kellach.

"That noise. It came from back by the pit."

Kellach rolled his eyes. "Are you going to start that again?"

"No, I heard something, too," said Calyssa. "It sounded like someone shouting. Listen."

They all stood in silence, straining to catch the slightest sound.

"Whatever it was," said Driskoll, "it sounded close."

"Then let's keep moving," his brother suggested.

Cautiously they continued past the stone walls of the hallway.

"It looks like a dead end up ahead," said Kellach.

Thrash wiped his forehead with the back of his wrist. "It's getting hot down here." As soon as the words left his lips, he jumped back like a startled cat, stomping on Driskoll's toes.

"Ow! Watch it!" The smaller boy leaned against the wall to take the weight off his trampled foot. "What happened?"

"A section of the floor shifted under my foot," said Thrash. "I thought it might be another pit, but I guess it was nothing. Unless . . . aw, for the love of mayhem."

"What?" said Driskoll, his voice rising sharply. "What is that supposed to mean?"

"I think I triggered another trap."

A hot draft blew over the little group, carrying with it the scent of a blacksmith's forge. The soft thud behind them could only be the sound of the door to the pit swinging shut.

"Uh-oh," said Lunk. "Door shut."

"Yes," said Driskoll. "But I don't think that's the worst of our problems."

Driskoll stood and faced the wall he'd been leaning against. "This wall is . . . moving!"

The others looked. Sure enough, the wall was sliding sideways. A glow like firelight flickered through the growing gap.

The opening kept expanding until it was almost ten feet wide. Calyssa held up the Eye and shined its light through the hole for a better look.

Beyond the opening loomed a small cave. Soot drifted between stalactites and stalagmites jutting from above and below like giant fangs. The stone of the uneven floor had a reddish hue, and a smell like hot ashes roiled out at them. The whole place seemed to shimmer with the heat pulsing from it.

The light from the Eye diffused until it was just a dim glow. Everyone squinted, willing their eyes to adjust faster, seeing only shadows and red sparks.

The sparks were drawing closer. In fact, they weren't sparks at all.

They were the glowing red eyes of . . .

CHAPTER

9

"Hell hounds!" Driskoll breathed, drawing his sword.

The ferocious canines stood tall enough to look him right in the eyes. At least a dozen of the brutes padded silently toward the cave entrance. The hackles on their broad shoulders stood on end, and black lips pulled back to reveal razor-edged fangs.

Against such a large pack, the group had no hope.

"We need to cover this entrance," said Thrash. "That will limit how many we have to fight at once. Fluffy, light us a torch and go get that door open."

This time, Calyssa didn't bother to argue about her name. She grabbed a torch from Driskoll's pack, lit it, and tossed it on the floor in the entrance. Then she raced back to work on the door.

As if responding to some signal only they could hear, the hounds crouched to attack, the closest one opening its mouth to breath fire at them.

Kellach lunged between Driskoll and Thrash, his finger extended toward the advancing hound. A ray of freezing air and ice blasted from his hand. It struck the nearest beast, cutting off its fiery breath.

The animal yelped and recoiled.

Lunk struck his fist against his chest, and a ripple of indigo light flitted over him. He shouldered his way in front of Driskoll and Kellach.

A second hound lowered its head, and a rush of flames poured from its mouth. Everyone fell back except for Lunk. The fire engulfed him, but the big healer stood fast, unharmed.

The other hounds hesitated.

"I can't get the door open!" Calyssa cried from down the hall.

Thrash looked over his shoulder at Driskoll and Kellach. "You two go help her! Hurry!"

Driskoll and Kellach raced back the way they'd come. Escape was their only hope. Even Thrash and Lunk couldn't hold out much longer against such beasts. Sooner or later, the hell hounds would win.

When the brothers found Calyssa, she had stuffed her dagger in between the door and the doorjamb. Driskoll quickly understood why. There was no handle on this side of the door, nothing to grab. They were trapped.

"Got any spells we can use?" Driskoll asked his brother.

"Not for this," said Kellach.

They began rooting through their packs, searching for something, anything, to get them through the door.

Suddenly the door flew open.

A shout echoed from somewhere out near the pit. "Come on! This way!"

The three of them rushed out onto the ledge.

"Thrash! Lunk!" cried Calyssa. "The door is open! Get out of there!"

The two half-orcs retreated to the doorway, their axe and mace the only things between them and the entire pack of hell hounds.

Thrash and Lunk kicked and swung at the snarling pack to keep them at bay, as Kellach pulled the door shut. The hell hounds slammed and clawed at it, but the sturdy wood held. Their angry howls rang eerily from the walls.

Shocked by their narrow escape, the group turned to thank their rescuer.

"Moyra!" Driskoll dropped his sword and clapped her on both shoulders. "Boy, are we glad to see you! See, Kellach? I told you someone was following us."

"How did you get here?" Kellach asked her.

"My mom made me help her at the market so I couldn't sneak off when it was time to meet you guys," said Moyra, "but I remembered enough of the map to find the mausoleum. From there it was easy."

"What do you mean, easy?" said Driskoll. "All those twists and turns—"

"Please!" She flicked her hand dismissively. "With the trail you people left in the dust, blind zombies could have found their way down here."

"Zombies?" said Lunk, scanning the area with a scowl.

"No, Lunk," said Thrash. "There are no zombies here."

"No zombies?" Lunk gave Moyra a stern look.

"It was just a figure of speech," she told him uneasily. She turned to Kellach. "Who are these guys?"

"This is Thrash, Kruncher's cousin," said Kellach.

Lunk let out a low growl. He wore the same pained expression they'd seen on him once before.

"I thought he looked familiar," she said. She turned a wary eye on the bigger half-orc. "But this one I don't recognize."

"That's Lunk," said Thrash. "Kruncher's little brother."

Again Lunk growled, the look on his face one of pure misery.

"Little?" said Moyra.

"Brother?" said Kellach and Driskoll together.

Driskoll eyed Lunk nervously. "Does he know we . . . ? I mean, will he . . . ? That is . . . why didn't you tell us that before?"

"Because I didn't think you twerps would keep bringing up you-know-who." Thrash jammed his greataxe back into its holster. "So from now on, knock it off. The more anyone talks about it, the more it upsets Lunk. And believe me, you do not want to see Lunk when he gets really upset."

Kellach quickly changed the subject. "But how did you get down here without springing the pit trap, Moyra?"

"Who says I didn't spring it?" A blush crept into her cheeks. "I did see it, and I tried to disable it, but I sprang it instead. I'm just glad you left that rope so I could get out of the pit."

"Oh, thanks for reminding me!" said Driskoll. He picked up his sword and sheathed it, then went to retrieve his rope. "Something tells me we may run into another trap or two before we get out of here. I can't afford to leave this behind."

"How about her?" Moyra nodded toward Calyssa, then frowned. "Hey! That's the girl who spilled dragon's draft all over me!"

"Yes, the girl we saw in the fortune-teller's Eye," said Kellach. "Her name's Calyssa."

"Fluffy!" Lunk said.

Moyra gave them a puzzled look.

"It's a long story," said Kellach. "We can fill you in as we go, once we figure out which way we're going."

Driskoll could tell Moyra didn't trust the newcomers. She watched them from the corner of her eye and never turned her back to them.

They all examined the two remaining doors. Except for the notches in the handles, they were exactly like the one they had just gone through. Ornate engravings covered both of them, the intricate designs unlike any they'd ever seen. The patterns seemed to shift, depending on how close or far away they stood. Moyra listened at each door but heard nothing.

"Well," said Kellach, "does anyone have any idea which way is south?"

The others shook their heads.

"Hmm. I figured whichever door was farther south might lead to the shortest way out of here," he said. "I guess we could just try door number two, unless someone has a better idea."

No one spoke up, so Kellach moved to the middle door, the one facing the slide. "Moyra you go first to look for traps." Moyra nodded and grasped the door handle.

"Everybody ready?" she asked. She didn't wait for an answer to swing the door open wide.

Driskoll gasped. What he saw rivaled any display in Val-Sages. Behind the door lay a small grotto with jagged walls of black crystal set at odd angles. The light from the fortune-teller's

Eye bounced off the glassy walls, ricocheting endlessly until the space lit up like a vast forest of moonlit gems.

Calyssa turned, sending the light from the Eye spinning and jittering. She dimmed the light, and the group saw that the walls formed a zigzag path that branched off in all directions.

The air here felt cool and dry, nothing like the sweltering lair of the hell hounds. They saw no immediate danger, sensed no trace of any living thing other than themselves. Yet the space felt crowded. The black crystal walls reflected their images back a hundredfold in a bewildering panorama. It reminded Driskoll of a hall of mirrors he got lost in once at the Promise Festival.

"That girl! . . . ," Calyssa exclaimed, pointing at one of her own images. When the girl mirrored her movements, she hesitated, confused. Her hand drifted to her face, then to the torque on her left wrist.

Moyra peered at the bracelet. "Calyssa, what's that design on your torque?" she asked, reaching toward it.

A burst of energy crackled in jagged white streaks from the bracelet. It blasted Moyra, sending her reeling backward to the brink of the pit. Lunk's hand shot out and grabbed her around the waist, pulling the teetering girl back to safety.

Lunk stood calmly, as if nothing had happened. The others hadn't realized the big half-orc could move with such speed.

Moyra's eyes were as round as wagon wheels. She jabbed her finger at Calyssa. "She's crazy! She tried to kill me!"

Calyssa looked as shocked as Moyra. "I didn't do it," she said. "I didn't do anything."

"Yes, you did," said Moyra, her eyes narrowing to angry slits. "Everyone saw you."

"But I didn't," Calyssa insisted. "The torque did it all by itself. You must have triggered something. The same thing happened to . . . before."

Kellach raised an eyebrow. "Who? Who did it happen to before?"

"It doesn't matter," she replied. "Someone tried to take the torque away from me, and it . . . stopped them."

"Then why didn't you tell me?" Moyra demanded. "If you knew I'd get hurt, why didn't you say something?"

"I didn't know. Really," said Calyssa. "I knew you were just going to look at it, so I didn't think anything would happen. I guess it's easier to set off than I thought. I'm sorry."

"Hmpf," said Moyra, unconvinced. "I wanted to get a closer look at it, because the dragons look just like the ones on our pins."

Kellach and Driskoll studied the bracelet, being careful to keep their distance. The twisted metal band appeared to be made of real gold. And Moyra was right. Both ends were shaped exactly like the rampant dragons on the pins Zendric had given them. The dragons faced each other, and between them they held a small silver crystal. "Where did you get that?" asked Driskoll.

Calyssa gazed at the bracelet. "I can't say."

"What?" Moyra exclaimed. "You'd better say, or we'll leave you here."

"Moyra—" Kellach began.

"All I can tell you is that it was given to me for protection," said Calyssa. "That's all you need to know. That, and keep your hands off it."

The girls glared at each other.

After a long moment, Thrash let out a deep breath. "The rest of you can stand around here arguing if you want," he said, "but we're out of here. Come on, Lunk."

Kellach laid a hand on Moyra's shoulder. "Come on, Moyra. It was just an accident. She's the one who got us all out of that pit, so we can't just leave her. Besides, we'll all stand a better chance of surviving down here if we stick together."

"Hmpf," was all she said. But she took her place beside Thrash as he moved toward the path.

CHAPTER

10

The path through the black crystal walls seemed endless. The constant reflections disoriented everyone, and every few steps they came to another fork in the trail. Driskoll had no idea how far they'd come or which direction they were heading, but he felt sure they hadn't made any progress. It wasn't long before they were hopelessly lost.

"It's a dead end," Moyra said for the third time, her voice dull and lifeless.

The others groaned. They all knew the drill by now. They turned around to retrace their steps. Before this, the trail had circled back on itself. Before that, another dead end. At least they hadn't stumbled upon any more monsters or sprung any traps.

Driskoll turned and began walking again. But after a few steps, utter blackness dropped on him. He stopped in his tracks.

"Hey!" Thrash's protest rang tightly from the crystal walls.

"What happened?" asked Driskoll, wishing he didn't sound so scared.

"Calyssa?" Kellach's tone was calm but concerned. "What happened to the light?"

No answer.

"Calyssa?" The concern in Kellach's voice rose a notch. "Moyra? Lunk?"

Still no answer. The only sound was from Kellach rummaging blindly through his pack.

"Lunk, are you all right?" Thrash's weapons clanked as he fumbled around in the dark.

Kellach spoke softly, and light flared as the waterskin slung over his shoulder glowed with the radiance of a spell.

The three boys looked around. They saw no sign of a trap or an opening, but the girls and Lunk were no longer beside them.

"This path seems narrower," said Kellach. "Did we take the wrong side of a fork just now, Driskoll?"

Driskoll backed up a few steps, dragging his hands along both walls. "I don't see any fork here."

Thrash tapped the flat of his axe against the wall. "You think the walls moved?" he asked.

Kellach nodded. "This one split our group right down the middle. Maybe the others can hear us on that side. Let me see your axe for a minute."

Thrash eyed him suspiciously, then held out the weapon. "Don't nick it."

Kellach took the greataxe with both hands, struggling a bit with the weight of it. Using only the flat side, he tapped a rhythm against the stone. When no response came, he tried again.

They waited a moment in silence. Nothing. Kellach passed the weapon back to the half-orc.

"So what do we do now?" asked Driskoll. "Stay put and hope they find us, or keep going and hope we find them?"

"I say we keep moving," said Thrash. "If this is another trap, I don't want to make it easy for whatever's trying to catch us. Besides, I have to find Lunk."

The brothers looked at each other and shrugged.

"You know," said Kellach, "now might be a good time to look at that map you took from the guy in the pit."

Thrash grunted, pulling the wadded paper from his pocket. "This doesn't mean you get a cut of the treasure or anything, but if it'll help us find Lunk . . . " He trailed off as he smoothed out the map against the wall.

It was small, no larger than a deck of cards. Lines stretched clear to its ragged edges, revealing that it had been torn from a larger map. There were no words. Just lots of squiggly lines running in all directions. In the top right-hand corner was a big red *X*.

"This isn't much of a map," Kellach said.

"Yeah, but there is an *X*!" Driskoll jabbed his finger against the crumpled paper. "That must be where we'll find the treasure. Maybe it will match up with some place we haven't come to yet."

"Let's just get going," said Thrash. He folded the paper and put it away.

"Lead on," said Kellach. "But let's stick close together."

The countless reflections of the boys flitting over the jagged black surfaces made Driskoll feel as though they were being watched. This, along with the threat of shifting walls and the long stretches of silence, began to wear on his nerves.

"Hey, look," Thrash said, pointing to an area up ahead. "The light isn't reflecting off anything up there. I think it's a way out." The half-orc broke into a jog.

"Thrash! Wait!" Kellach called after him. He and Driskoll hurried to catch up. They had almost reached him when he slipped through a glassy black surface. What the half-orc had stumbled into wasn't a way out. It wasn't an opening at all. It was some vile cross between liquid and crystal.

Thrash turned back toward them even as he slid deeper into the crystal wall. His face stretched in a silent scream of horror. All around him, ghostly reflections loomed within the crystal, pawing at him and wailing soundlessly. The big warrior only had one arm and one leg free by the time the brothers reached him, and he was sinking deeper.

Kellach lunged for his hand, and Driskoll grabbed Kellach around the waist. Together they pulled, but Thrash was slipping away. More reflected faces swarmed toward him. Driskoll threw a glance over his shoulder but found no one there to cast the reflections. Then he noticed his own reflection was missing from the shiny surface and so was Kellach's. What were all those faces? Remembered reflections? Trapped souls? Driskoll shuddered and pulled harder on his brother's waist.

"Driskoll!" shouted Kellach. "Grab his arm and keep pulling!"

Driskoll let go of his brother and latched onto Thrash.

Kellach uttered a few strange words and flung his arm out toward the oily wall. A blast of light shot from his fingertip and

66

struck the wall next to Thrash. The wall shivered and shimmered. The reflections shrieked.

Driskoll heaved on the half-orc's arm. Thrash came tumbling out of the wall with a slurping sound, knocking Driskoll over and landing on top of him.

"Oof!" Driskoll shoved against the bigger boy's shoulders, trying to push him off. His hands landed in something slimy. "Eww!"

Thrash rolled to a sitting position and furiously swiped his hands over his face. He was covered in some kind of muck. It smelled faintly of vinegar.

"Are you all right?" asked Kellach.

Thrash patted himself down. "I think so," he grumbled.

"I meant my brother," Kellach said.

Driskoll pushed himself up off the floor with a groan. "Yes," he said, "I'm fine. What is that thing?" He eyed the black wall warily.

"I'm not sure," said Kellach. "It's some kind of living wall. Someone has been messing around with some very powerful magic down here."

"Is that how we're all going to end up?" asked Driskoll, wiping the slime from his hands onto his jacket. "Nothing left of us but our reflections?"

"No," said Thrash, heading back the way they'd come until he found another path. "We're getting out of here. If Lunk runs into anything like that, it'll scare the bejeebers out of him. I have to find him." Determination rang in his tone and words, yet he moved a bit less quickly than before.

Driskoll suspected the wall had scared the bejeebers out of

Thrash, but he thought he'd better not mention it. No sooner had the brothers set off after the half-orc than the reflections of Kellach's light spell suddenly vanished.

"Kellach, do you want to go with another spell, or should I get my lantern out?" asked Driskoll.

No answer.

"Kellach?" Driskoll fought back his rising panic. "Thrash?"

The only sound was the echo of his own voice from much too near. The blackness around him felt close, like a coffin. Were the paths trying to suffocate him? Had he walked into one of those walls like Thrash did? "No, no, no, no, no," he said, his jaws clenched firmly together to keep his screams inside.

"Driskoll?" The voice came from right behind him. At the same time, a light flared, revealing someone standing toe to toe with him.

"Ahhh!" Driskoll nearly jumped out of his skin. "Ahhh!"

"Driskoll! It's me!"

His mind finally cleared enough to see that the someone in front of him was him. A wall had appeared there, and he was screaming at his own reflection. He whirled around to find Calyssa behind him. For a moment, all he could do was gape and gasp for air.

"Are you all right?" she asked.

"Don't sneak up on me like that!" he shouted.

A massive paw clamped down on his shoulder, and he let out another yell.

"Be nice to Fluffy," said Lunk.

"Be nice? Be nice?" he ranted. "You two scared me half to death!"

Lunk scowled down at him. His grip on Driskoll's shoulder tightened.

Driskoll's knees began to buckle. "Ow! Oh, you want me to be nice to Fluffy. Well, sure. I can do that. Why didn't you just say so? Nice, good Fluffy." He gave Calyssa a very gentle pat on the head.

Lunk didn't turn him loose.

"It's all right, Lunk," said Calyssa. "He didn't mean to yell."

Lunk smiled a lopsided smile at her and let Driskoll go.

Driskoll shook his head. "I'm getting the heck out of here." He headed down the first path on his left, then stopped. "I'm glad you guys are all right."

Calyssa fell in behind him, and Lunk followed. "Have you seen any of the others?" she asked.

"I was with Kellach and Thrash." He told her what had happened. "What about Moyra?"

"She was with us, but we got separated." She paused. "Your friend doesn't like me much. Does she?"

"She's always a little suspicious of people at first," Driskoll said, not wanting to hurt the girl's feelings. "And I think the shot she took from your torque scared her, and that made her mad. Besides, you can't really blame her for wondering about you."

"What do you mean?"

"Well, you came into a seriously dangerous area alone, unarmed, and with no supplies." Driskoll grinned. "Let's face it. That's just not normal."

Calyssa was quiet for a moment. Then she said, "Well, when

I went back to get the map from that guy, he made it sound like this would be easy."

"That's weird," said Driskoll. "He told me to bring friends."

The path widened, and he dropped back beside Calyssa.

"So how did you and the others get on Thrash's bad side?" she asked. "I thought he was going to kill you back in ValSages."

"He probably would have, if you hadn't distracted him." Driskoll laughed. Then he grew serious. "We'd better save that story for another time, though. I don't want to upset . . . Lunk?" He glanced to see whether the big half-orc had been paying any attention to their conversation. But Lunk was gone.

"Oh, no!" Calyssa's hand clapped over her mouth. "I hope he's not alone!"

"Me too," said Driskoll. "But he's a big guy. He'll probably manage better than any of the rest of us."

"Yeah, but he might get scared. And Thrash will kill us if anything happens to him."

"Hey, it's not our fault," said Driskoll.

"I don't think that will matter," said Calyssa. "I was listening to them in the pit, before they knew I was there, and Thrash is really different around Lunk. He actually seemed . . . nice."

"Nice?" Driskoll's eyebrows shot up. "Thrash?"

"I was shocked too. But I could tell Thrash doesn't just take care of Lunk. He really cares about him. They're like brothers."

"That's hard to imagine. If you had known Thrash before—"

"Ooh, look!" Calyssa interrupted. "I think I see an opening up ahead!"

"Be careful!" said Driskoll. "That's what Thrash thought right before he got caught in that slimy wall."

But they both pressed on with renewed energy. And Calyssa was right. A few steps farther and the path opened out into a small grotto.

The grotto they had started in.

The grotto with the door back to the pit.

Emerging from another path were Lunk, Kellach, Moyra, and Thrash. Everyone let out shouts of relief. But their joy at finding each other again quickly gave way to frustration.

Thrash pounded his fist against the stone wall. "We've been wandering in circles!"

"It's not possible!" Moyra wailed. "I can't believe this!"

Lunk took off his pack and dug out a piece of jerky. He went out the door and sat on the ledge, his legs dangling into the pit. He proceeded to munch as if he'd found the perfect location for a picnic.

Driskoll's stomach let out a loud rumble. He glanced at the others, then decided the heck with it. He reached into his own pack and pulled out a bag of nuts and dried fruit.

The others all did the same. All, that is, except Calyssa. She carried no pack and, therefore, had no food.

"Do you want some nuts?" Driskoll asked her, holding out the bag.

Calyssa took a handful. "Thanks. I forgot to bring anything to eat."

No food, no water, no weapons, nothing. Just the fortune-teller's Eye. Nobody in their right mind came down here completely unprepared. What was she thinking? Driskoll wondered.

"Well, there's only one door left," Kellach said. "Do we want to try these paths again—see if we missed something? Or should we see what's behind door number three?"

"The door," everyone said in unison. They all laughed. No one wanted anything more to do with the crystal paths anytime soon.

Kellach grasped the door handle and looked over his shoulder at the others. Without his having to ask, they all nodded that they were ready. He pushed the handle of the third and final door.

CHAPTER

11

The door swung open to reveal a straight, rough-hewn tunnel sloping deeper into the earth. The kids followed it for nearly half a mile, finally coming out into a huge cavern.

The place was as wide as three tournament fields and twice as long. The ceiling soared upward like a grand cathedral built by giants. Stalactites and fissures covered it, the light from below casting them into eerie relief. Something seemed to be moving up there, but it was impossible to say for sure.

The chamber stretched away to either side, but the floor ended abruptly about thirty feet in front of them. A deep chasm severed the room from one end to the other, cutting off their side from the opposite wall.

Calyssa focused the light from the Eye on the movement on the ceiling. At first much of the surface seemed covered in a black blanket with something writhing underneath. Then individual creatures became visible.

Bats. Thousands of them. Their near-silent squirms and flutters filled the chamber with ghostly whispers.

73

Kellach cringed.

"What's the matter?" asked Calyssa.

"He hates bats," Driskoll answered.

Thrash laughed and shook his head. "Afraid of bats! What a sissy."

There appeared to be no immediate threat, so the group ventured a bit farther into the chamber. As they approached the chasm, they noticed something directly in front of them.

Set into the floor at the chasm's edge was a single black crystal tile, roughly the size of a large book. The crystal looked like the kind they'd seen in the dead-end paths. Etched upon it in elegant, silver lettering were the words "To Promise."

Thrash and Calyssa stopped several feet short of the chasm's edge. The others moved up beside them for a better view. No one seemed eager to get close to that deadly drop.

"Do you think there's a path down to the chasm floor from here?" asked Kellach. "Maybe just below the lip of this ledge?"

"I don't know," said Thrash. "Why don't you go lean over the edge and look."

"Maybe there used to be a bridge to the other side," said Moyra.

Driskoll listened distractedly as the others discussed a number of scenarios and possible approaches to the situation. An updraft from the chasm brought cooler air with it, sending chills up his arms. He looked past the mysterious tile, down into the abyss. The seemingly endless void made him feel lightheaded and a little queasy. He forced his gaze upward to try to regain his balance. That's when he noticed the door.

Across the chasm, a sheer cliff wall formed the far side of the chamber. It rose from the unknown depths to the craggy ceiling with hardly a crack or an outcropping. Set high in the cliff face was a door. It had no landing, no stairway, no ladder, not even a handle. The only indication that it was in fact a door was its shape and size.

That, and the elegant, silver lettering etched upon it. The door bore a single word: Promise.

"What do you suppose that means?" he asked, pointing.

For a few moments, no one spoke. They all just stared.

Finally, Kellach broke the silence. "Promise . . . ," he said, rubbing his chin, "Before the Sundering of the Seal, Curston was called Promise. It could be the way out."

"Hey, if this is the way out, we'll take it." Thrash took a step toward the tile. "Come on, Lunk. Let's get out of here."

Lunk's hand lashed out and caught his arm. "No, Thrash. Not good."

Thrash turned to his cousin. "We have to try it, Lunk. It may be the only way home."

"But . . . what about the treasure?" Driskoll asked.

Thrash pulled the crumpled map from his pocket and handed it to Driskoll. "I don't want to owe you guys anything. Since you got me out of that wall-thing, I'm giving you this. If you actually find any treasure, I expect a finder's fee. Deal?"

Driskoll figured this was the closest thing to a thank-you he'd ever get from Thrash. With a glance at Kellach, he accepted the map.

"Deal," Driskoll said.

"Now let me go, Lunk," Thrash said. "It's time to go home."

"Not good," Lunk said again. He did not release his cousin's arm. "Stay together."

Thrash sighed. "Only one of us will fit on that tile at a time, Lunk. You don't want to wander around down here till we all get killed, do you?"

Lunk frowned. Still he held on to his cousin.

"I have an idea," said Kellach. "What if we tie a rope around your waist, Thrash? That way, Lunk can hold on to you and feel like we're all still together. It'll be safer that way anyway. I mean, he does have a point. It could be another trap, or you could slip, or the ledge could give way under your feet . . . "

"Thanks," said Thrash. "Walking toward a bottomless hole in the earth wasn't hard enough without all that in my head."

Kellach grimaced. "Sorry."

Driskoll uncoiled his rope once more and passed it to Thrash. Meanwhile, Moyra checked the tile thoroughly but found no traps.

Thrash secured one end of the rope around his waist and handed the other end to Lunk. "Okay, Lunk?"

Lunk tied his end around his waist and looped it around his thick forearm. "Okay, Thrash."

Thrash took a deep breath and let it out. Then he squared his shoulders and strode toward the tile. Gingerly he placed one foot on the tile.

With a flash the tile turned silver.

Thrash jumped back. At the same time, Lunk hauled on the rope. Thrash stumbled backward into Driskoll, Moyra, and Lunk. The four of them tumbled to the ground in a heap.

"Ow!" said Moyra from somewhere in the pile. "Get off me, you big lunk."

"Lunk is down here," said Lunk from the bottom of the pile.

Eventually they sorted themselves out. Calyssa pushed up her sleeve as she reached to haul Driskoll to his feet, and once again he caught a glimpse of the scar on her forearm, the one he'd seen when she was talking to Zhigani. It was shaped like a skull and crossbones. Driskoll noticed his brother looking at it too.

Calyssa followed their gazes to her arm, and she quickly pulled her sleeve back down to cover the scar.

Kellach turned his attention to helping Thrash up. "Did you see anything below the ledge?" he asked. "Any sign of a path?"

"No," Thrash said. "I didn't really get a chance to look around."

"Hey!" Driskoll said. "The tile is black again. Do you think it's a trap?"

Kellach scanned the area. "I don't know. It doesn't look like it triggered anything. But we could still turn back if you think it's too dangerous."

"Nah," said Thrash. "Let's try it again. It'll be all right."

He and Lunk checked the rope. The others gave them room. Again Thrash stepped onto the tile.

Again the black tile flashed to silver. This time, Thrash kept his foot on it.

Nothing else happened. He took a quick glance over his shoulder, then moved his other foot onto the tile.

Right in front of Thrash there was another flash. A new black tile appeared, floating just beyond the chasm's edge and a step higher. Nothing supported it, and it didn't move. It simply hung there, as if it were waiting.

"What do you see from there?" asked Moyra.

"Just that thing," he replied, pointing at the tile.

"No stairs hugging the cliff?" asked Driskoll. "No ladder leading to a passage below us?"

"Nothing," said Thrash. "Not even the bottom of this chasm. Wait. There is something down there."

"What is it?" asked Calyssa.

"More bats. Lots of them. All down the cliff face, as far as I can see."

"Oh, great," said Kellach.

Thrash glanced back at the others. "Brace yourself, Lunk," he said. "And keep a tight grip on that rope. I'm going to try that next tile."

The others scarcely dared to breathe. Lunk dug in his heels and leaned away from the ledge, leaving just enough slack in the rope for his cousin to take one more step. Kellach grabbed on to Lunk's belt for extra support.

Thrash lifted his foot. He swayed slightly, waving his arms to regain his balance. Gently he set his foot onto the floating black tile.

The black tile flashed to silver. Thrash shifted his weight onto it, lifting his other foot from the tile on the ledge.

The tile held him. A new black tile appeared, floating just beyond the silver tile where Thrash was standing and a step higher. At the same time, the silver tile on the ledge vanished.

"Uh-oh," said Lunk.

"Uh-oh?" Thrash craned his neck to see what had happened. Again he wavered slightly and quickly turned forward to catch his balance. "All right. I'm going to try one more step and see what happens."

He stepped up onto the next black tile. Again the black tile flashed to silver, the tile he had been standing on vanished, and a new black tile appeared just above and beyond the one he now stood on. He was now two steps above and two steps out over the chasm.

"It looks like a one-way road out," said Moyra.

Lunk stood near the chasm's edge, frowning. "No, Thrash," he said. "Not good."

"Yes, this is good, Lunk. I'll go first, then you." Thrash went up two more steps.

"No!" Lunk shouted. He drew the rope taut, pulling Thrash off balance.

Thrash swayed back and forth on the little tile, windmilling his arms to keep from falling. When he had steadied himself, he spoke in a much higher voice than usual. "Lunk! Don't pull the rope! Do you want me to fall?"

"No. We stay with Fluffy," Lunk insisted.

"No," Thrash said, "we have to get out of here. It's not safe with her. Someone's trying to kill her. She just wants to use us as walking shields."

"I do not!" Calyssa snapped.

Thrash ignored her. "Now Lunk, I'm going up these steps, and you're going to follow. Okay?"

"No." The big half-orc folded his arms and stuck out his chin.

Kellach cleared his throat. "Um, Thrash? There are a couple of other points to consider."

They all looked at him expectantly.

"First, whoever got us into this—if they're even still alive—is only expecting to tangle with Driskoll and Calyssa, not all six of us. The other thing," Kellach continued, "is that we've obviously missed something."

"What do you mean?" asked Moyra.

"We've run into a pit trap, trick doors, hell hounds, dead ends . . . and one easy way out. It can only mean one thing." He looked around triumphantly. "There's something down here. Something important. Something big enough for someone to go to all this trouble to keep people away."

Driskoll, Moyra, and Calyssa looked at one another. One by one, they nodded their agreement. They must have missed something. There had to be something down here. But what?

When Thrash didn't answer, Kellach added, "Unless you're too chicken to stay."

"Chicken!" Thrash roared.

"Chicken?" said Lunk, his face lighting up.

"Not that kind of chicken, Lunk," his cousin growled.

"You and Lunk would get a third of whatever treasure we find, instead of just a finder's fee," Kellach pressed.

Thrash shuffled his feet in a slow circle till he faced the ledge. "Wizard-boy, you'd better hope we find a *lot* of treasure."

The half-orc's gaze flicked to the open space gaping below him, and he squeezed his eyes shut. "Lunk, get ready," he said. "I'm going to jump back there."

Driskoll could well imagine what was going through the young warrior's mind. Though only a few feet separated him from the ledge, the abyss yawning around that space made crossing it seem inconceivable. The slightest mistake could spell disaster. To make matters worse, the tile Thrash stood on was so small, it gave him no room for a running start. He'd have to make a two-footed hop. The only thing working in his favor was the fact that the tile was slightly above the ledge, giving him a small, but hopefully adequate, boost.

"On three," said Thrash. He wiped the palms of his hands on his pants. "One. Two . . ."

CHAPTER

12

"T hree!" Thrash swung his arms forward and leaped as if his life depended on it, because it did.

At the same time, Lunk hauled on the rope, and Kellach hauled on Lunk's belt. As Thrash's boots hit the ledge, the other two boys backpedaled to take up the slack in the line.

Thrash cleared the gap with plenty of room to spare, but when he landed, a few stones shook loose from the edge and tumbled into the chasm. The faint rattle and bounce of their long descent echoed upward, sounding hollow and amplified.

Thrash stepped away from the edge, and the others let out a sigh of relief. He and Lunk untied the rope and handed it back to Driskoll.

"What was that?" Calyssa asked sharply.

"What was what?" asked Moyra.

"Shh!" Driskoll hissed. "I heard it too."

Kellach rolled his eyes. "Are you two going to start with that again?"

"Uh-oh," said Lunk.

All heads turned toward him. In the brief pause, they all heard it. It sounded like dogs shaking water from their fur. Or banners waving in a strong breeze.

And then came other sounds. High pitched sounds, like tiny, squeaky wheels. Like shore birds fighting over scraps. Like . . .

"Bats!" cried Driskoll.

By the thousands they came, spewing up from the chasm like water from a fountain, a very large, very angry fountain. They formed an enormous black shroud across the cavern, their fluttering wings and piercing shrieks echoing and rising to a deafening wall of sound. And still they kept coming.

"The debris from the ledge must have fallen on them and set them off," Moyra shouted over the tumult. "Let's get out of here!"

Moyra and Calyssa stumbled through the door first. When the whole group made it back out to the pit area, they pulled the door shut behind them. Only a few bats squeaked out with them, and those flew through the hole in the ceiling and up the chute.

Thrash writhed around the ledge, flailing his arms and gibbering. "Gah!" he cried. "Yeek!"

The others, watching his bizarre dance, started snickering, even Kellach. No one expected such a tough guy to be afraid of bats. Or to act so weird about it.

At last Thrash tugged his shirt collar away from his neck. A bat fluttered out of his shirt and flapped up the chute after the others. The half-orc shuddered. Then he glared at the others. "Nobody says a word," he warned.

Driskoll bit his lip and turned away to keep from laughing out loud.

"All right," said Thrash, trying to reclaim his dignity. "Where do we find this treasure?"

"Let's go over this whole area again," said Kellach, "try to figure out what we missed. We concentrated on the three doors before, so I'm thinking we should take a closer look at these walls. Maybe all these carvings mean something."

Carefully they searched the encircling walls and the elaborate patterns that covered them, looking for anything that seemed out of place.

Driskoll pulled out the scrap of map, comparing it to the designs on the doors and walls, hoping for a clue. He noticed the others rolling their eyes when they saw what he was doing, but he felt sure the map must be important. Otherwise, why would the dead man have bothered with it? It still didn't match up with anything they had encountered, so he folded it up and put it away again.

"I think I found something," Kellach said after much searching. He was examining the wall between doors one and three. "It's harder to see here under the slide, so this detail is easy to miss. See how the patterns are the same on all three walls, except this section right here?"

He pointed to a design that looked like a flower. On the other two walls, the petals stood out from the background in high relief. On the wall between doors one and three, however, the petals lay closer to the background in low relief.

"What do you think?" he asked. "Another trap or something new?"

Moyra examined the lower petals. "There's definitely something here, but I can't tell what it does."

"Only one way to find out," said Thrash.

The others agreed.

Kellach pressed on the lower petals. There was a click, and the petals raised to match the others. With a low scraping of stone on stone, two sections of the wall parted to reveal a secret passage.

"Yes!" said Driskoll, beaming. He headed for the passage.

"Careful," Moyra warned. "There could still be more traps in there."

The secret passage looked much like the others, standard stone corridor. This one was quite short, though. Moyra stepped inside the doorway.

"I thought so," she said. "Look. There is another trap here."

"Can you disarm it?" asked Kellach.

"I'll try." She reached into her tool kit and pulled out a metal pick with a hooked end. Kneeling near the entrance, she began working at a device in the wall.

Driskoll peered impatiently into the room beyond. It must have been used as children's quarters some time ago, judging by the size of all the furniture. A rough-hewn table and four chairs occupied the center of the room, and four cots lined the walls, two on either side. The back wall held a small fireplace.

But who would keep children in a place like this? Deep underground, behind hidden doors . . .

A metallic *ping* brought his attention back to the matter at hand. Moyra was backing away from the entrance.

"I think I got it," she said.

"You think?" said Thrash.

A whirring sound cut off further discussion. Suddenly, an iron gate crashed down in front of them, barring the entrance to the room.

Dust and rust scattered through the air.

Thrash waved his hand in front of his face to clear the air. "So you think you got it, huh?" he repeated, scowling at Moyra.

"Yeah," she said. "But I could be mistaken."

"Hey, at least we're making progress," said Kellach. Orange and gray silt drifted from his hair as he tilted his head forward and gave it a gentle shake.

"Progress?" said Thrash. "What progress? You call this progress?" He clanged the handle of his greataxe around in one square of the iron gate, playing it like a musical instrument.

"Of course," said Kellach. "The traps we've seen so far were designed to keep us in, so we'd either escape or die trying. But these bars are supposed to keep us out, which means what we want is in there."

Thrash turned to Driskoll. "Does he always talk this crazy?"

"Pretty much. Yeah."

"No, he's right," said Moyra. She had taken a small mirror from her pack. She was holding it through the gate and using it to look at the walls on the near side of the room. "There's a treasure chest over in the corner to the left."

That got everyone's attention. They pressed forward, trying to peer through the gate.

"I knew it!" Driskoll gloated. "I told you we'd find treasure down here!"

86

"Hey, you're squishing me." Moyra squirmed between Lunk and Driskoll to get out of the way.

"So how do we get in?" asked Thrash, his face close to the gate. When no one answered, he turned to Kellach. "Well?"

Kellach shrugged and turned to Moyra.

Moyra shrugged and turned to Thrash.

Thrash clenched his fists and made a noise that sounded too much like a growl. "Oh, what good are you people? I have to do everything myself."

Moyra's jaw dropped. She raised her finger, ready to give him a piece of her mind.

Driskoll laid a hand on her arm and shook his head. "He's wrong," he murmured so only she could hear, "but let's not make him angry on top of that."

She glanced at Thrash's muscular form. Her mouth snapped shut, and she made a show of searching for a release switch to raise the gate.

"Come on, Lunk," said Thrash. "Give me a hand with this gate." After holstering his weapon, he crouched with his back to the gate, hands gripping one of its lower bars.

Lunk did the same. When he was ready, he nodded.

The two cousins struggled to rise, straining against the heavy gate. Muscles flexed and cords stood out on their necks and arms. Their grayish skin took on a tinge of red.

Inch by agonizing inch, they raised the gate more than a foot. Not a lot, but enough for the other four to slide under it. Once there, they all grabbed the bars from the other side so that Thrash and Lunk could slide through.

"You first, Lunk," said Thrash between clenched teeth.

Lunk didn't argue. He almost never did. He simply dropped to the floor and rolled under the gate. It dipped a bit when he let go, but the others held it long enough for him to grab it again from the other side.

"Ready, Thrash," he said.

Thrash dropped and rolled. As soon as he had cleared the gate, he yelled, "Go!"

Everyone let go of the bars, and the gate crashed to the floor once more. The smaller members of the group blew on their blistering hands.

"Whew!" said Calyssa, flexing her fingers. "I hope we don't have to do that again."

The others looked uncertainly toward the chest. Carved into its closed lock were two dragons snarling at each other.

"We did it! It's the treasure the fortune-teller showed us!" Driskoll exclaimed, starting toward it.

"Easy, little brother," said Kellach, putting a hand on his shoulder. "Better let Moyra check for traps first."

Thrash let out a snort of contempt. "Yeah, like that'll do us any good. She couldn't disarm a trap if you gave her a full set of instructions and a magic . . . disarming . . . thingy."

"Oh, yeah?" said Moyra. "Well, at least I know how to put a few word thingies together. Your only so-called skill is that you were born huge."

"Got you in here, didn't I?"

"All right, all right," said Calyssa. "Can we just get on with it?"

Moyra nodded, but without much conviction.

Thrash had obviously hit a nerve with his ridicule. Moyra

88

had been botching a lot of traps lately, and having it thrown in her face like that couldn't improve her confidence. "Come on," Driskoll whispered in her ear. "You'll show that big oaf."

At that, she smiled and went to work. She pulled out her kit and selected a few tools.

The other five edged toward the far corner of the room. If Moyra noticed, she didn't comment.

Carefully she examined the chest, then sat back on her heels. "Well, guess what," she said.

"Hm, let me see," said Kellach. "Another trap?"

"Oh, yeah. And this one's a real piece of work."

"Do you think you can handle it?" asked Calyssa.

Thrash snorted and rolled his eyes. He managed to keep his remarks to himself this time, though.

"I already did," said Moyra. She made a face at Thrash, then lifted the lid of the chest. Driskoll winced, half expecting an explosion or some other unpleasant surprise.

Moyra let out a gasp. "I can't believe it!"

"What?" the others chorused, rushing across the room to join her. "What is it?"

"It's empty!"

The others looked over her shoulder into the chest. Sure enough, there was nothing in it.

"That doesn't make any sense!" cried Driskoll, dropping to his knees beside her. He felt around in the trunk for anything their eyes might have missed.

She shook her head. "Someone must have gotten here before we did."

"Our treasure!" Thrash snapped. "Somebody stole our treasure!

If I ever get my hands on them . . . "

"What about the gate?" said Calyssa. "Is there at least a release switch in there?"

"That's the weirdest part," said Driskoll. "There's no treasure and no release switch. So why wasn't this trap already sprung or disabled?" He drummed his fingers in the bottom of the trunk in thought. The low tapping boomed like a marching army in the quiet room.

Kellach frowned at him. Something wasn't right.

Driskoll frowned as well. They looked at each other a moment, trying to figure out what it was. At the same instant, their faces registered surprise and understanding.

"The bottom!" cried Driskoll.

"It's hollow!" said Kellach. He began fiddling with the bottom of the trunk, pushing, pulling, sliding. At last he pushed on one edge of it, and the opposite edge popped up.

"A false bottom," said Moyra. "Somebody sure went to a lot of trouble to hide something."

"I can't see through all your big heads," said Thrash. "What's under there?"

Kellach set the false bottom aside and examined the contents of the secret compartment. In the middle of the trunk sat a small, glass sphere. "Now that's odd."

"What?" Thrash demanded. "What is it?"

"Well, it looks a lot like that fortune-teller's Eye Calyssa has," he said.

"Is it valuable?" asked Thrash.

"Is it food?" asked Lunk.

"I have no idea."

"Hey, look," said Driskoll. "There are markings carved into the real bottom of the chest." He reached in to pick up the strange object, so he could get a better look at the markings. It wouldn't budge. "This thing's attached," he said.

Kellach grasped the object and gave it a twist, trying to pull it free. It lit up in his hand, and he jumped back. The clear globe clouded, then filled with black-and-silver designs. Whirring and clicking noises came from under the chest. The grinding of distant gears rang down the corridor.

The six companions cast about in alarm, wondering what kind of trap they'd sprung this time. Lunk gave voice to what was going through all their minds.

"Uh-oh," he said.

CHAPTER

13

With a deafening squeal, the iron gate rose. As it receded into the ceiling, the sounds of gears and pulleys died out.

"See?" said Kellach. "Now we're on the right track. I knew there was something more down here."

"More what?" said Thrash. "We still haven't found any treasure."

"I don't think the treasure was *in* this chest. I think this chest *leads* to the treasure." Kellach examined the orb and the markings around it carefully. "Okay, let's see . . . "

Lunk continued to stare at the sphere. He seemed convinced the shiny object was food.

"I think I've got it," said Kellach. "Dris, give me your lantern."

When his brother handed him his lantern, Kellach lit it. "We don't want to risk running into the hell hounds, and we don't want to take the exit, so let's focus on door number two, the crystal paths. I need for all of you to go open that door and wait right there. But be ready for anything."

"Like what?" said Thrash. "What are you going to do?"

"See these four symbols carved around the sphere?" said Kellach. "A straight line, crossed lines, a triangle, and a square. I think they represent the three doors plus the secret door."

"One line, two lines, three lines, four lines," said Driskoll. "Makes sense."

"When I turned this sphere," Kellach continued, "a design formed inside the glass. It reminded me of a kaleidoscope. I think if I turn it some more, I'll eventually get a design that matches the symbol for door number two, the two crossed lines. They form an *X*, and *X* always marks the spot for treasure."

"Okay," said Calyssa. "Suppose you get the design you want. Then what?"

"That's what you're all going out there to find out."

The others exchanged uneasy glances.

"What if you set off something in here?" said Driskoll. "I'm going to stay and watch your back."

Kellach hesitated, then nodded. The rest shuffled out to do as Kellach asked.

"Let me know when you're ready," he called out to the others.

The brothers waited, listening as the group got into position out on the pit ledge and opened the door to the crystal paths. At last, they heard Thrash's call.

"Ready!"

Slowly Kellach turned the sphere, watching the pattern inside it change as he moved it. "If I can just get the right design," he said as he worked, ". . . like that!" He released the sphere, eyes wide in anticipation.

Glowing black lines crossed in the middle of the sphere, and silver bolts of light flowed from them to the matching mark carved into the bottom of the chest. This time, however, no whirring and clicking noises trickled up from under the chest.

"Are you sure that's the right design?" asked Driskoll.

Before he could answer, the startled exclamations of the others sent both boys sprinting out to the pit. Kellach grabbed the lantern, and Driskoll drew his sword as he ran.

"What's wrong?" asked Driskoll, skidding to a stop beside the others, who were standing side by side in front of the open door. Then he noticed their expressions. They didn't seem frightened or dismayed, as he'd thought. They looked amazed, curious. Following their gazes, he turned to the crystal paths.

The black, reflective surfaces had vanished. In their place, neat rows of silver crystal were shifting, combining to form a single straight path retreating into the distance.

"They just . . . changed," said Thrash. "Like the tiles leading across the chasm, only all at once."

Kellach put out the lantern and passed it back to Driskoll. "Did you see anything else?" he asked. "Any signs of life? Or danger?"

"No," said Moyra. "Nothing. The black crystal walls all just turned silver and started moving around. Do you know where this leads?"

"No," said Kellach. "But what do you say we find out?"

No one had any arguments with that plan. Eagerly they set off down the silver passage.

This path was nothing like the others they'd been in. The

walls were all smooth and seamless, like polished steel, but they didn't show any reflections at all. Instead of straight lines and right angles, this path curved and meandered.

Secretly Driskoll worried that the passage would change shape behind them, closing off their exit, swallowing them like a giant throat. He forced the thought from his mind and focused on the path ahead.

The smooth, clear passage did make travel easy, though. He had to admit that. Within twenty minutes or so, they had covered a good mile.

That's when the path opened into another cavern. This chamber was almost as large as the one with the Promise tile. It was roughly bowl shaped, and they were standing in the bottom of the bowl. The walls were pocked with dozens of openings, presumably leading to many more pathways.

Dominating the far wall, hewn in stone, a towering, lifelike dragon snarled down at them. Its head and claws lunged out from the wall, as if the monster had burst from the very earth and it was only a matter of time before it freed itself entirely.

Everyone froze. Not a sound filtered down from the dragon or the pathways.

Driskoll broke the silence. "It could take weeks to explore all these paths!" His voice sounded loud in the wide space.

"Maybe months," said Kellach. Though he spoke more softly than Driskoll had, the odd shape of the chamber amplified his voice and carried it to the farthest corners.

"Or maybe not!" said Driskoll. He pulled the folded map from his pocket. "Maybe this is where this map comes in!"

Moyra looked over his shoulder as he scoured the piece of

map once more. "Hey, let me see that a minute," she said, taking the paper from his hand.

She turned it to look at it from another angle, then turned it again. "Aw, Driskoll! This is from a map of the Galleria in ValSages!"

"What?" he cried in disbelief.

The others let out a groan.

She held it in front of him. "Look. Here's the path to the Inner Sanctum, only the plaza and the game hall have been torn off. And this *X*? That's not treasure. It's the Swashbuckler!" She showed him a few more points of reference, and it was clear she was right.

"Well, so much for map number two," said Kellach.

"Yeah," said Moyra, "this whole thing was just a ValSages scam. We should go back. We've already been gone too long. We're going to be in enough trouble."

Thrash scowled, still scanning their surroundings. "It would really stink to give up after all this, but . . . " He looked at his cousin.

Lunk stood, calm as usual, regarding the great stone dragon. He appeared content to go along with whatever decision the others came to.

"The rest of you can turn back if you want," said Calyssa, "but I'm going on."

"What?" said Moyra. "Are you crazy?"

"You'll never make it down here on your own," said Driskoll. "You don't even have any supplies."

"I managed before I met any of you, and I'll manage when you leave."

"You managed to fall in a pit and get hurt," said Driskoll. "What will you do next time without Lunk there to heal you?"

"Or when you bump into some more hell hounds, or something even worse?" Moyra added.

"I'll take my chances," Calyssa replied. "Someone tried to kill you. I mean us. And someone's been trying to keep us out of here. I'm not just going to let them get away with that. Are you?"

Driskoll started to answer, but Kellach stopped him. "You won't change her mind. Calyssa *has* to go on. She can't go back, because she has a secret. Isn't that right, Calyssa?"

The others looked from Kellach to Calyssa and back. Calyssa shifted uncomfortably under their gazes, but she said nothing.

"Secret?" said Thrash. "What kind of secret?"

Kellach looked at Calyssa, but she wouldn't meet his eyes. "Do you want to tell them, or shall I?"

CHAPTER

14

Calyssa tossed her long ponytail from her shoulder. "Tell them what?" she asked lightly.

Kellach only flicked his gaze down to the sleeve covering her right forearm.

Calyssa hesitated, then pushed her sleeve up, revealing the angry scar marring her otherwise smooth skin. It was shaped exactly like a skull and crossbones. Above the picture, tiny words stated: "Property of the Swashbuckler."

"That's a game hall slave's brand," said Kellach. "Calyssa is the escaped slave the ettin was searching for in ValSages. If she returns, it will be to slavery, prison, or even death."

The others gaped.

"So, there's a bounty on her head?" said Thrash, a greedy gleam springing to his eye. "How much?"

Driskoll sputtered, "You can't turn her in! She saved your life!"

Thrash shrugged. "If Lunk and I hadn't shown up, she might still be in that pit. Or maybe she'd be hell hound chow. Besides, she's a dangerous criminal. Right, Fluffy?"

Calyssa watched him from the corner of her eye. "That's right, so keep your distance."

"I knew we shouldn't trust her!" Moyra turned on Thrash. "And you armed her!"

"But she helped us," Driskoll protested. "She didn't have to pull us out of that pit. She could have just left us there."

"Could she?" said Moyra. "I'd say we helped her at least as much as she helped us."

"You're right." Calyssa's voice was soft in the face of their hard accusations. "You did help me, but that's not why I helped you first."

"Then why did you?" asked Thrash.

She shrugged. "Because you needed it. Because I could."

"So why were you a slave?" Moyra wanted to know. "What did you do?"

"I . . . I don't know." Calyssa usually kept pretty calm, but now she seemed nervous. She kept fidgeting, and she wouldn't look anyone in the eye.

"What do you mean, you don't know?" asked Moyra. "You had to have done something! Or was it so horrible you just won't tell us?"

"No! It's just . . . " Calyssa's hands knotted so tightly her knuckles turned white. "I really don't know! I don't know what I did, or what they think I did. I don't know how I got to Val-Sages. I don't know where I came from. I don't even know who I am!"

With this last admission, her lip began to quiver. Tears welled in her eyes, but she blinked them back. "My memories only go back a few weeks. One day, I woke up in the game hall slaves' quarters, and I couldn't remember a thing. Not even my own name! One of the slave girls felt sorry for me, kind of took me under her wing, showed me the ropes. She gave me the name Calyssa, after her own sister. She taught me some acrobatic tricks, so I could be a performer and avoid some of the nastier jobs slaves have to do. She's the one who taught me to protect myself too."

Once she started talking, the words continued to tumble from her like water bursting through a floodgate. "Then yesterday, she disappeared. Nobody would talk about it. I just knew something bad had happened to her, and I didn't want whatever it was to happen to me. So I ran."

The others listened in silence. Moyra and Thrash seemed skeptical. Driskoll and Kellach remained a bit more receptive, though not entirely trusting. Only Lunk seemed unaffected by her tale.

"I know you probably don't believe me," she said. "I probably wouldn't believe me either, but it's true. I didn't remember a single thing. Until today."

"Wait a minute," said Moyra. "I thought you just said you don't remember anything."

"And I don't. Not really." Calyssa looked at them one by one, as if gauging how much she should tell them. "Today I started getting these flashes of people and events. Like when I said that all I could tell you is that this torque was given to me for my protection. That's exactly what I remembered about it. Not who gave it to me, or when, or anything else.

"At first I thought the flashes were visions of some kind, but now I'm pretty sure they're bits of memories. They feel somehow familiar anyway. Only, they're so fragmented, I can't make any sense of them. And I don't know who the people are, so I don't even know if they're important at all. But at least now I have some hope of figuring out who I am and what I'm supposed to be doing."

She held up the fortune-teller's Eye. "See, when Zhigani gave me this, she told me I wasn't always a slave. She said, 'The Eye will help you find your past and your path.' Those were her exact words. She used the Eye to show me the way to the ruins and told me to wait for her at the entrance to the catacombs. I didn't get a chance to find out any more from her, because the game hall thugs were after me. I had to run. So I waited where she said, but she never showed up."

"Okay. Hold it," said Thrash. "Are you saying you never went back to the con man and got a map?"

Calyssa bit her lip and shook her head.

He pointed a finger at her. "So you lied."

Her nod was almost imperceptible.

"So why should we believe anything you tell us?" he asked.

"Because I'm telling you the truth now! I couldn't tell you all this back then. I didn't know if I could trust them." She waved a hand toward Kellach and Driskoll. "And I *knew* I couldn't trust you."

"Hey!" the half-orc protested.

"Oh, come on, Thrash," said Moyra. "You have to give her that one. A minute ago you were ready to turn her in for the reward."

"Yeah? And who said I changed my mind?"

Moyra rolled her eyes. "What I want to know is, can we trust this Zhigani person? I mean, she sent you into that pit. Maybe she's the enemy. Maybe she was working with the guy with the maps."

"She didn't send me into the pit," Calyssa corrected. "She told me to wait for her in the catacombs. It's possible she set me up, but I don't think so. I think something happened to keep her from meeting me. Maybe I just feel connected to her because she knew about my missing memories. But would an enemy give me this?" She looked at the Eye, as if it might give her an answer.

"What about that?" asked Kellach, indicating the Eye. "Have you tried to use it for anything other than providing light?"

"What do you mean?"

"Well, Zhigani told you it would show you your past and your path. Right? So, has it shown you anything?"

She frowned at it. "No, but I don't have any idea how to use it."

"Then how did you get light from it?" asked Driskoll.

"That happened by accident. When I got to the ruins, I wasn't sure I remembered how to get to the meeting place. I said something like, 'Now which way do I go?' and poof! It lit up the path. Then when I was waiting for Zhigani, I just wished for light, and it worked."

"Have you tried wishing for anything else from it?" asked Kellach.

"No," she replied. "Magical wishes can backfire so easily, I didn't want to take any chances messing around with it. But I guess I could try it now. What should I wish?"

"If you're not lying about your missing memories," said Moyra, "ask it to show you your past. Zhigani said it would, right?"

Calyssa held the orb up at eye level. "Show me my past," she said.

The Eye went dark.

The entire cavern went dark with it.

"Did it break?" asked Lunk.

CHAPTER

15

Give that light back!" snapped Calyssa.

The Eye complied, its steady glow dazzling after the absolute darkness.

"Well so much for the Eye," Driskoll said.

"This thing is worthless!" Calyssa said. "I wish it would show me something useful."

Suddenly the light dimmed. Inside the Eye a blur of scenes appeared. First, it showed Zhigani hurrying on foot along a busy road. Driskoll didn't recognize the place until the fortune-teller reached the city gates of ValSages. Then the image in the Eye drew back to reveal the con man tracking Zhigani, following her from a distance into the city.

The scene dissolved like cloud candy in a rainstorm, and another took shape. This one showed the con man and a tiny stranger beside the pit trap. With his neatly trimmed beard and enormous nose, the stranger resembled a gnome, but he was shorter than most of that race and completely bald. Both men's faces were red and contorted with rage. They appeared to be shouting.

Again the image dissolved, and a third took its place. In this one, Zhigani, now wearing an eye patch in place of the Eye, crept along one of the paths in the chamber where the viewers now stood. She glanced over her shoulder, then went out one of the openings into the central chamber with the dragon. Almost immediately, the bald gnome entered the chamber and followed her, leaving just enough distance between them to keep from being seen.

The Eye went momentarily dark. When it brightened again, it was clear once more.

"Wow!" said Kellach. "It worked!"

"Yes," said Calyssa. "But did any of it mean anything to you? Did anybody recognize the little bald man?"

The others shook their heads.

"No," said Driskoll. "Did you?"

"No," she replied.

"All right," said Kellach. "Let's see how much we can figure out. The con man was tailing Zhigani, so they probably weren't friends."

"The bald man argued with—and maybe killed—the con man and followed Zhigani," said Moyra, "so does that make him her friend or her enemy?"

"Well, at least we know the con man and the bald man were enemies," said Thrash.

"Not really," said Calyssa. "Just because they fought doesn't mean they were enemies. Maybe Zhigani killed the con man, and that's why the bald man was after her."

"More importantly," said Kellach, "what are they to us? So far, Zhigani seems to be a friend. We know the con man was an enemy. And now I think I know why he gave Driskoll the map. He must have seen him talking to the fortune-teller and figured he was her friend."

"The fortune-teller talked to tons of people," said Moyra. "He couldn't have given maps to all of them. He didn't even give maps to the two of us."

"That's true," said Kellach. "He must have recognized Driskoll's pin, just as Zhigani did. But then why did he try to sell maps to Calyssa and Thrash?"

"We were both talking to Driskoll when the man tried to sell him the map," Calyssa said. "He may have thought I was a friend of Driskoll's. He knew Thrash wasn't, but maybe he just didn't care if an extra body wound up in the pit."

"Mm," said Moyra nodding. "What about the bald man, then? Enemy?"

Kellach rubbed his chin. "It certainly looks like it, since he was tailing Zhigani. But I don't think we can know that for sure. Maybe you should ask the Eye for more information, Calyssa."

She looked doubtful. "I don't know what good that will do."

"What do you mean?" asked Driskoll.

"Well, none of this really helps us, because we don't understand what we've seen."

"True," said Kellach, "but maybe you weren't specific enough. Or maybe it can't give that information for some reason. Zhigani said it would show you your past and your path, right?"

"She said it would help me *find* my past and my path," said Calyssa. "That might mean something different than showing them to me. Maybe we shouldn't be messing around with this thing. I mean, it's obviously very powerful, and we obviously have no idea what we're doing."

"Mm. You have a point." Kellach hesitated. "But maybe we should try one more thing."

"What?"

"Zhigani said it would help you find your path, so see if you can get it to do that."

Calyssa gazed at the Eye, its flawless surface giving away no hint of its purpose or the extent of its power. "Show me my path." She spoke the words in a rush, as if to get it over with before she lost her nerve.

A blast of white light streamed from the Eye. It blazed across the cavern to engulf the stone dragon. Suddenly, the Eye winked dark again, then resumed its clear, even glow.

The others turned to Calyssa expectantly. She stared up at the great stone beast, part wall, part statue, then took a step toward it. "I don't see any path," she said at last. "Do you?"

The others groaned in disappointment.

"I hate to say it, but that one was right," Thrash said, hooking his thumb toward Moyra. "Let's get out of here."

"No, wait. I just thought of something else," said Kellach.

None of the others showed much interest. They had had enough. They were ready to give up.

"Calyssa," the apprentice persisted, "when did you get those flashes of memory you mentioned?"

"Which ones?"

"Any of them. The first one."

"I'm not sure . . . " Her brow wrinkled in concentration. "The memory about the torque came when we opened the doors to the crystal paths. And when I first saw the cavern with the black tile, it felt like some other place, some place where I belong, and yet I don't. But I can't picture the place, it's just a feeling. I'm sorry. I know that doesn't help."

"So you're saying the memories are triggered by something? Like, something you see or feel," said Kellach.

She started to nod hesitantly, then her eyes flew open wide. "Yes! But not only then. I just remembered when I felt that first flash! It was in the pit. When Lunk healed my ankle, I got this image of something that looked a lot like this." She held up the Eye. "And then I saw Zhigani pushing me."

Moyra frowned. "Pushing you?"

"Not to harm me," Calyssa explained quickly. "She was pushing me, like . . . I don't know. I can't remember any details, but I feel certain she was pushing me to help me. Pushing me away from danger or toward . . . something else."

"And that was the first memory to come back?" asked Kellach. When she nodded, he said, "And you said that came when Lunk healed your ankle, right?"

She nodded again.

"Maybe if Lunk casts the same spell on you again, he can bring back some more of your memories." Kellach turned toward the big healer. "Can you do that, Lunk?"

Lunk had been staring up at the paths and openings, absently scratching his back with his mace. Hearing Kellach address him brought his attention back to the discussion. "Do what?"

"Can you cast that healing spell on Calyssa again? The one you used to fix her ankle."

Lunk looked down at Calyssa's ankle. "I made Fluffy's ankle better already."

"Yes, we know," said Kellach, "but we want you to cast the spell again."

"Fluffy's ankle is not hurt now."

"No, we know that," said Kellach, the patience draining from his voice. "But we want you to cast the spell again anyway."

Thrash chuckled. "You can argue with him all day, twerp. You won't get anywhere. How can he heal what isn't hurt?"

Lunk took Kellach's shoulders in his big hands and looked into his eyes. "Fluffy's ankle is okay, twerp," Lunk said slowly, as if explaining to a child.

Kellach smacked his hand to his forehead. "Ah, this is hopeless."

"I could bloody her nose," Thrash suggested helpfully. "That would give Lunk something to heal."

Calyssa glared at him. Then she turned to his cousin. "Lunk," she said, taking his hand and placing it on her head, "can you make this better for me?"

Lunk angled his head to the side, as if listening. "Yes, Fluffy," he said after a moment. "I can make it better."

Kellach threw his hands in the air. "That's all I was asking!"

Lunk grasped Kellach's wrist and pulled his hand to Calyssa's head. "This is not Fluffy's ankle, twerp," he explained.

"Yes. Great." Kellach's voice dripped with sarcasm. "Thanks for clearing that up. Now can we just get on with it, please?"

Calyssa tapped the healer on the arm to get his attention again.

Lunk touched his finger to the girl's temple and muttered something in orc. A violet halo appeared around her head. The aura expanded, turning deep indigo. Then it winked out of sight as he lifted his finger. "Better, Fluffy?"

There was a faraway look in Calyssa's eyes. She blinked a few times, then looked up at Lunk. "Yes, better. Thanks, big fellah."

Lunk patted her on the head and went back to looking around the walls of the chamber.

"Well?" said Driskoll eagerly.

"Well," said Calyssa, "I got back a few more fragments, but nothing that really made any sense to me."

"What did you see?" asked Kellach.

"Some girl," said Calyssa. "Her face seems really familiar, but I don't know who she is. And then there was a throne . . . and then . . . just this feeling that I'm running out of time, that we need to hurry."

"Hurry where? To do what?" asked Moyra.

Calyssa pointed to the stone dragon. "But I don't remember what I need to do here. It's so frustrating. I feel like it's on the tip of my tongue . . ."

She took a step toward the dragon, then another.

"That's it!" she cried.

"What?" said the others all together.

But Calyssa was running the last few steps to the dragon's enormous snarl. Cringing, she reached between its fangs and grasped its forked tongue. She pushed and pulled, but it wouldn't budge. Then she shifted it to one side, up, back, and then to the other side. "That's all I remember," she said, dusting off her hands and stepping back to see whether she'd accomplished anything.

High above them, one of the dragon's stone eyes disappeared, replaced by a glowing swirl of energy. Calyssa scrambled up the dragon's claw and leg to get a closer look. The beads around her neck swung, and the Eye clinked against the stone face. She tucked it under her tunic and kept climbing, silhouetted against the strangely gleaming eye of the dragon.

"Calyssa, wait!" Driskoll called after her.

"No, this is it!" she called back. "This is my path!" She climbed onto the stone cheek, gazing into the dragon's eye.

"What do you see?" asked Kellach.

"Nothing," she replied. "I—"

She never got a chance to finish the thought. Two pairs of hands reached out from the misty eye and grabbed her. Before she could even cry out for help, they yanked her through the glowing barrier.

In an instant, she was gone.

CHAPTER

16

"Fluffy!" Lunk's voice rang out, filled with despair. Before anyone could move to stop him, he ran up a path that led to the dragon's eye. "Fluffy, wait!" he cried, and he leaped into the energy field after her.

"Lunk!" Thrash sprinted up the path after his cousin, pulling his greataxe from its holster as he ran.

"Stop!" Driskoll yelled. "Thrash! It must be a magic portal of some kind. It's probably another trap."

Thrash had reached the portal. He paused in front of it just long enough to reply. "I know. That's why I have to get Lunk out of there."

Kellach, Driskoll, and Moyra exchanged uneasy glances and came to a silent agreement. "Wait for us," yelled Kellach.

The three of them drew their weapons and joined Thrash in front of the portal. When the half-orc stepped through the energy field, the others were right behind him.

As Driskoll passed through the portal, a tingling crawled over his entire body, like a hand waking after having the circulation cut off. The hair on his arms and the back of his neck stood on end, and his eyes filled with brilliant silver spots. The passage seemed as if it would never end, but it actually only took an instant. Then he was through.

And he was wishing he weren't. His ears popped, and his body shuddered in reaction to being teleported. But that was the least of his worries.

The others were all there, trying to shake off the effects of the portal as he was. They had stepped into a tiny room with seamless stone walls, as if the place had been carved from solid bedrock. Two small iron doors faced each other in the far corners. The table, chairs, and cabinets were all quite small, like the furniture they'd seen in the secret room with the empty chest. Only now Driskoll understood that the furniture wasn't built for children.

Eight little men with brownish-gray skin surrounded Driskoll and the others. Their wiry frames and ample noses suggested they were gnomes, but these were even shorter and a bit fairer than most. They wore gray leather uniforms with a snarling dragon insignia on the sleeves. They seemed to be soldiers or guards of some sort. All of them had eyes like blue ice.

Though the little men did not even reach as high as Driskoll's shoulder, they clearly had control of the situation. One of the men held a dagger to Calyssa's throat. A second man stood over Lunk's prone form, a spear tip at his back.

Looking down at these men felt strange to Driskoll, as if he'd suddenly grown into a giant. He was used to looking up at people. How could such tiny men have taken Lunk down? And how did they manage it so fast?

He found out soon enough. A third little man, this one wearing a short sword with a jewel-encrusted hilt and scabbard at his hip, barked something in an unfamiliar language. A blur slipped past Driskoll, streaking among him and the other three. In and out it wound, back and forth. A wave of dizziness washed over him just from watching it.

And then it stopped. The blur came to an abrupt halt, and Driskoll could see it was a fourth little man. He'd never known anything could move so fast! No wonder Lunk's strength had proven no match for these creatures. He couldn't hit what he never saw coming.

Driskoll and the others didn't see the speedy guard coming until it was too late, either. They now stood tied loosely to one another with their wrists bound tightly behind their backs.

Thrash snarled and struggled, trying to burst the bonds that held him. But it was no use. The cord binding them appeared to be as extraordinary as their captors.

"Who are you?" Kellach managed at last. He turned toward the one with the jeweled weapon.

"Captain ask question!" the little man replied in common tongue. His thick accent made him difficult to understand. "Until he come, you quiet."

He snarled in his strange language at his underling.

The guard that had bound them spun on his heel and zipped over to a tall cabinet against the back wall. A drawer opened with a squeal, and he removed a slender red wand. The wand appeared to be carved of solid ruby set with a black crystal on top.

Driskoll started to protest, but Kellach gave him a nudge. His lips pursed silently into the universal signal to keep quiet.

Once more, the guard moved between them in a blur, this time tapping them each with the wand.

Driskoll's tongue felt fuzzy, and his ears buzzed.

"What did they do to us?" he asked Kellach.

The underling saluted the guard with the jeweled sword. "All set, Lieutenant Flim," he said.

Driskoll blinked. This little man spoke with no accent, but the sounds coming from his mouth didn't match the movements of his lips.

"Ah," said Kellach. "Translation spell."

"Silence!" shouted the one called Lieutenant Flim. He turned to his men. "Throw the intruders in the dungeons!"

Driskoll sneaked a look at his brother, hoping he had come up with a plan to get them out of this mess. At a slight shake of Kellach's head, the younger boy's heart sank.

The little men exchanged awkward glances.

Lieutenant Flim glared at them, his face turning red with anger. "Well? What are you waiting for?"

The one with the wand cleared his throat. "I don't think they'll fit in any of the cells," he said. His mouth went on and on as if he were reciting an epic poem, but only those few words came out.

"Then shrink them!" Flim shouted. He stamped a tiny foot for emphasis. "Or must I handle everything myself?"

"Yes, sir! I mean, no, sir. I mean, we'll get right on it, sir." He zipped back to the cabinet and exchanged the ruby wand for a stout, blue one. This wand appeared to be carved in sapphire. At the top of it sat another black crystal. Once more, the guard moved between them in a blur, tapping them each with the new wand.

At the wand's touch, Driskoll's skin crawled and felt wrinkly, as if he'd gone swimming and stayed in the lake too long. His view shifted from seeing the tops of the men's heads to looking at them at eye level to craning his neck up at them. He looked over at his friends; they had all been shrunk as well.

The guards bound Lunk's and Calyssa's hands behind their backs. Lunk went into a frenzy when they took his mace. "Clobber!" he bellowed. "Give back Clobber!" He kicked and tried to rise, but the guard above him jabbed the spear point into his back.

"Easy, big fellah," said Calyssa.

He craned his thick neck to look at her, his features a mixture of fury and agony.

"Big magic," she added softly.

His gaze flicked to where the Eye dangled, hidden under her tunic, then back up to meet her eyes. He simply looked at her for a moment. When he dropped his head, he appeared calm and cooperative.

Four of the guards led the captives through the door on the right. They marched down a hallway decked in a series of dazzling murals and into a stairwell. The four who were tied together had to move carefully to avoid pulling each other off balance and tumbling down the stairs.

The guards herded them along a seemingly endless series of stairs and passageways. There were no murals or decorations of any kind in these lower levels, only torches set in sconces at wide intervals. The path had so many turns, the corridor so many branches, that Driskoll soon became convinced they'd never find their way back out. He focused on staying calm until finally they reached the dungeons.

In a room with a door on one side and an open doorway on the other, the guards turned their prisoners over to two more guards. The new guards removed the prisoners' packs and dropped them onto a table with their weapons. Then they led their captives through the open doorway to yet another corridor beyond.

Doors of iron bars flanked this hall. Side corridors led off to the left and right. The jailors pushed the prisoners into a cell and slammed the door behind them. The six of them barely fit in the tiny space. The screech of metal on metal as the key turned in the lock sounded horribly permanent, like a death sentence.

As the echo from the guards' boots retreated back up the corridor, Driskoll turned to face his friends.

"Well," he said, "it looks like we need a plan."

"Right. A plan would be good," said Moyra. "We could start by . . . um, trying to figure out who these people are."

Calyssa's head snapped up. "Svirfneblin."

"Gods bless you," said Moyra.

"That wasn't a sneeze," said Calyssa. "That's what they're called: Svirfneblin. They're gnomes who live in great cities deep underground."

Kellach nodded slowly. "I've heard of them, but I don't know that much about them. What else can you tell us?"

She sighed. "Not a thing."

"Okay," he said. "Well, have you remembered anything else that might help us out here?"

Her black ponytail swung as she shook her head. "No. Stray things keep popping into my head, but none of it fits together.

Like when I saw the snarling dragons on the guards' uniforms, all I could think of was one word: *king*. That's it. Just *king*."

"The king is dead!" crowed a voice from somewhere down the hall. "Long live the sovereign!"

CHAPTER

17

L unk jumped at the sudden sound. He spun to scowl at who-ever was responsible.

Calyssa moved beside him, and the others stepped up behind to look over her shoulder. The corridor and doorways stood empty. "Who's there?" she called quietly.

"The king is dead! Long live the sovereign!" the voice repeated merrily.

"Who are you?" Calyssa asked in a hushed tone. "Come out where I can see you."

They saw movement behind the edge of the cell door that was kitty-corner from theirs. At the same time, they heard a faint jingle.

"Come on," Calyssa coaxed. "We won't hurt you. We're locked up too."

A pale face popped into view through the other cell door. Over it drooped a two-pointed hat, one half gold and the other violet, each with a bell attached at the end. Dark circles ringed icy blue eyes above a beard grown scruffy. The face disappeared

119

behind the doorjamb again. But his clothes were unmistakable.

"A jester!" exclaimed Driskoll.

The face appeared again. "Surely you jest!"

Calyssa frowned. "What madness is this? No one jails a jester."

"Stuff and nonsense!" said the jester. "Though not necessarily in that order."

"I beg your pardon?" said Calyssa.

"Nonononono!" said the jester. "Mustn't beg, child. It's rude."

"He's loony," said Thrash.

"Of course he's loony," said Driskoll. "Jesters usually are."

At that, the jester drew himself up and gave Driskoll an imperious stare. "Some of us *always* are."

Then he leaped into the air, clicked his heels and clapped his hands. "Lords and ladies. Boys and girls. Friends and callous, thick-headed, evil louts," he said in a booming, theatrical tone. "The Voices Inside My Head Choir proudly presents a special matinee performance of its highly acclaimed 'Songs from the Dungeons in B Sharp'."

A bellow rumbled down the corridor from the guardroom. "Pipe down, y'old nutter!"

The jester bowed low in the guards' direction. "Thank you," he said. "Likewise, I'm sure."

With that, he straightened his tattered, diamond-patterned suit and mounted an imaginary horse. Then, galloping around his cell, he began to sing.

Loony, loony Jester!
An avalanche for brains!
The goose has people-pimples,
And no princess remains!

Hey!

"I said leave off with that racket, ye clockwork buffoon,"
yelled the guard.

The jester didn't miss a beat. Daintily he lifted an imaginary
skirt and pranced in circles.

The king has kicked the bucket
His tortoise and his hare.
If monsters get his firstborn
It's neither here nor heir!

Come on! Everybody join in!

"Don't make me come down there!" the guard shouted.

The jester only raised his invisible skirt higher and kicked
his legs in the air.

Kill her, hide her, give her
A potion in her stew
While fencing with your bathtub!
This verse sure stinks! Pee-ew!

Okay! Now let's hear just the girls!

A chair scraped against the floor. "Right!" said the guard. "That does it."

The jester held his arms out, first to one side, then to the other, swaying like seaweed.

The toad is in the pudding.
The crown is off its head.
If it would only ask them
She'd tell me what you said.

Beautiful! Now all the boys with salamanders for ears!

"How many times do I have to tell you?" The guard's voice drew closer.

Now the jester flapped his arms like a duck, alternately rising up on his toes and crouching down in time with his music.

An ale drank too much cleric!
We're running out of time!
So get me out of Mios
before I lose my toe-stubbing dirt clod hourglass potato rickets earwax sunflower capsize fork knife spoon and . . . flea circus!

Thank you very much! We'll be here all eternity. Good night, Dungeons!

The guard had reached the jester's cell. His torch threw the jester's face into a macabre play of light and shadow. Jabbing the butt of his spear through the bars of the door, he whacked the bowing, grinning jester on the knuckles. "No more matinees!"

The jester yelped and stuck his injured fingers in his mouth. "Mm!" he cried, taking them back out and looking at them as if seeing them for the first time. "Tastes like chicken!"

"Quiet, you!" snarled the guard. "One more word about the royals, and I'll tell the rats where you've been hiding."

"No!" the jester whimpered. He dropped to his knees and clasped his hands pitifully beneath his chin. "No, please! Not the rats! I'll be good!"

"Good isn't good enough. Just you be quiet."

"Oh, yes!" he whispered. "I'll be quiet. Quiet as a . . . "

Whatever else he said was lost. He crawled into the far corner of his cell and sat on the floor. With his knees pulled to his chest, he rocked back and forth, murmuring to himself.

The guard grunted in satisfaction and retreated up the corridor. He hadn't even wasted a glance on his other prisoners. Darkness overtook the jester's cell once more.

Calyssa waited until the guard was gone. Then she called out quietly. "Jester?"

No reply came from the darkened cell. Only the faintest of mutterings carried on to indicate that the jester was still there at all.

CHAPTER

18

"Jester?" Calyssa called again. "The king is dead!"

She waited a moment, then turned to the others. "Well, if I can't get a 'Long live the sovereign!' out of him, I don't think he's going to respond to anything."

"What was all that about anyway?" Moyra wondered.

"Who could keep track?" asked Thrash. "It all just sounded like the rantings of a loony to me."

"I can remember most of it," said Driskoll. "Maybe all of it."

Calyssa gave him a skeptical look. "How could you remember all of that after hearing it just once?"

Driskoll shrugged. "Things like stories and songs just seem to stick with me." To demonstrate, he recited the first verse.

"'. . . no princess remains,'" Calyssa repeated. "That could be something. The girl I remembered, the one whose face seemed so familiar? I think she's a princess. That seems right."

Driskoll narrowed his eyes in concentration. "And 'The king

has kicked the bucket' is just another way of saying the king is dead. He repeated that a few times, so that seems pretty important to him."

"Either that, or he just likes the way it sounds," Moyra added. "This is a crazy person we're talking about. Remember?"

"True," said Kellach, "but it might be the very reason the jester is here."

Calyssa's jaw dropped. "You don't suppose he murdered the king, do you?"

"They'd have probably executed him on the spot, if that were the case." Kellach squirmed in his bonds. "But that part about a 'firstborn' seems to fit in with the topic of a dead king, or maybe with the part about the princess."

Moyra shrugged. "I guess it's possible. Then that part about the crown might go along with the stuff about the king or the princess too."

"Or does he mean the crown is off the toad's head?" said Driskoll.

"Ugh! This is impossible!" said Moyra.

"She's right," said Thrash. "You're wasting time. You should be working on getting us out of here."

"Hey! Wait a minute!" said Driskoll. "One of the last things the jester said was 'get me out of Mios.' Didn't Zhigani introduce herself as 'Zhigani of Mios'?"

"That's right!" said Kellach.

Calyssa's face brightened. "Mios! I know that word. It's a name, a realm. It must be this realm."

"See! At least we got something out of all that." Kellach looked intently at her. "Anything else?"

She frowned, trying to remember more. "Not really. Unless—"

"Someone's coming," said Lunk.

Everyone froze.

"How many of them are there?" asked Kellach.

"Three."

"Quick!" Kellach hissed. "Everyone look scared."

"I think we can manage that," said Driskoll. He could hear footsteps approaching in the corridor.

Three men arrived at their cell door. One was Lieutenant Flim, who turned a key in the lock on their cell door. The second had bulging muscles, carried a whip with a barbed tip, and wore an executioner's hood. The third was the bald gnome the Eye had shown them.

Calyssa gasped. "It's—"

Kellach nudged Driskoll hard, pushing him into the girl. She stumbled slightly when he bumped into her, and she turned to see what was going on.

"Silence, prisoners!" barked Flim. He swung the door open and jutted his chin into the tiny chamber. "You speak when Captain Kruiq here orders it, and only then."

"Thank you, Lieutenant Flim. You and the Breaker may wait for me in the guard chamber."

"Yes, sir." The lieutenant handed the keys to Kruiq and left with the Breaker. Their footfalls echoed down the corridor.

Kruiq stepped into the doorway as his underlings retreated down the hall. His voice was soft yet menacing at the same time. "I'm curious as to what the prisoner had to say. 'It's' . . . what?"

Calyssa hesitated. She looked from Captain Kruiq to Kellach and back.

"It's . . . such a relief that you're here," Kellach improvised. "That's what she was going to say. There seems to have been some big misunderstanding, and we're hoping you can help us get it sorted out."

"Really? Is that what you were going to say?" he asked Calyssa. The mockery in the captain's tone made it plain he wanted to toy with his captives, ensnare them with their own words. "How fascinating! You must tell me all about it. But there's something else I must discuss with you first."

The captain studied each of his prisoners in turn. An uncomfortable silence grew. He continued to scrutinize them, but still he did not speak.

Driskoll began to wonder whether the captain had asked a question, and he just hadn't heard it. He fought back the urge to speak, to say anything to break that dreadful silence.

"Good," said the captain at last. "Now that we've dispensed with the pleasantries, you can tell me where the heir has gone."

Six blank stares met this demand.

The captain waited patiently, all the while watching their every expression. "Come now," he prompted at last. "Don't be shy. First one to answer correctly goes free."

The prisoners exchanged uneasy glances. Kellach spoke for all of them. "We don't know," he said.

"Rubbish!" snapped the captain. "Don't play games with me, boy. You'll find it more painful than anything you can imagine."

Kellach blinked. "No, really. We don't even know who you're talking about."

"Don't lie to me!" the captain snarled. "You were seen talking with the seeress!"

"The seeress . . . you mean Zhigani?"

"Aha! So you admit knowing her!"

"We only talked with her once," said Kellach. "Is she the heir? Because we have no idea where she is now."

"Of course the seeress is not the heir!" Captain Kruiq shouted. His face turned red as lava.

For a moment, no one dared to speak.

"Very well," said the captain, regaining his composure. "Perhaps you've just forgotten. Fine. No problem. We'll just change the arrangements. Maybe that will help jog your memory. That massive fellow in the hood was The Breaker, our leading expert in questioning and executions. First one to reveal the whereabouts of the heir will be the only one not turned over to him."

The captives gasped in disbelief and outrage.

"You can't do that!" Driskoll cried amid the others' angry protests.

The captain chuckled. "Oh, so now you all want to talk at once, eh? Isn't that typical."

Kellach quieted the others. To the captain, he said, "What if we tell you, but you find the heir isn't there anymore?"

"Oh, that's different. Then you all die."

Kellach gave the others a long look to let them know he was up to something. "Well, that's it then. When should we expect to be executed? At dawn?"

"Ah, but it's not quite that simple." The captain's thin smile had returned. "Before we start executing people, we have to attend to the formalities."

"Formalities?"

"Of course. Before we kill you, we have to make sure you really have no information. And the only way we can be certain of that is to torture you." The captain gave a little sigh. "Sadly, The Breaker will have to torture you to death. To make sure you're not just holding out, you understand."

"All right," said Kellach. "You leave us no choice. We'll talk."

CHAPTER

19

The other five gaped at Kellach. They started to protest, but he overrode them.

"We'll talk," he said, "but only all together as a group, and only to the person in charge."

Captain Kruiq favored him with a condescending gaze. "And just who do you think is in charge?"

There was a pause. Driskoll had no idea who was in charge, and he knew Kellach didn't either. If Kellach made a wild guess, the captain would know he was bluffing.

"Look," said Kellach at last. "You're wasting time. You have two choices. One, you can take us to the person in charge immediately. Or two, you can torture us to death, in which case you get to explain to the person in charge why you killed the people with the information you need. So what's it going to be?"

Kellach and Kruiq traded hard stares, each waiting for the other to blink.

"Flim, Breaker," called Captain Kruiq, still not blinking, "prepare the torture chamber."

Then Kruiq waved his keys in front of Kellach's eyes to make him flinch. "You're fools to resist. But you'll have plenty of time to reconsider. The Breaker has been known to torture people for days before killing them."

He slammed the cell door, locked it, and stormed off toward the guardroom.

Thrash glared at Kellach. "Are you nuts? The only thing worse than being tortured to death is being tortured to death *slowly*. Thanks a lot!"

"Oh, come on," said Kellach. "I just bought us some time to escape."

"Escape how?" Moyra demanded. "There are guards swarming all over that portal. We'll never get past all of them."

Driskoll's heart sank. He wondered whether he would ever see his father again. He wished he were back home with him right now.

"I'm not planning to escape through the portal," Kellach said. "Besides, even if we could get through the portal, what's to stop these guys from coming after us? Don't you get it? We'll never get out of this mess until we give them what they want: the heir."

"If Captain Cranky can't find the heir, how will we?" said Driskoll. "What can we do?"

"First," said Calyssa, "we escape."

She proceeded to fold herself in half, face to her knees, dropping her hands to the floor and stepping back over the bonds around her wrists. When she stood up, she had her hands in front of her. Though her wrists were still bound, she could move her fingers enough to untie the knots at Moyra's wrists.

Moyra's jaw dropped. "Why didn't you do that before?"

"Because if the captain caught me, he'd have put me into something I really couldn't get out of."

When Moyra's cords fell away, she untied Calyssa's. Then the two girls set about freeing all the boys. As they struggled with the bonds, they worked out a plan.

"All right," said Moyra, as they all stood there rubbing their wrists. "Assuming we do get out of here, where do we look for this heir person?"

"And how are we going to know the heir if we find him?" asked Thrash. "We don't even know what he looks like."

From across the corridor, the jester whispered, "Follow the leader! The walls tell all!"

"He definitely knows something," said Calyssa. She moved to the cell door. "Jester? Follow what leader?"

No reply. "Jester? Which walls tell all?" She called quietly to him several times, but he would say no more.

"Maybe he means those murals we saw in the corridors near the portal," said Kellach. "I only got a glimpse of them, but they were very detailed. Maybe they hold a clue to where the heir went."

"But those murals must have been there before the heir went missing," said Calyssa. "How could they tell us anything about something that happened after they were created?"

"I don't know," Kellach admitted. "But do you know of any other walls that might tell us anything? I mean, at this point, what else do we have to go on?"

"It seems pretty farfetched." Calyssa turned to the others.

"I can't believe I'm saying this," said Moyra, "but I think

we have to do it the jester's way. Except we don't know how to get back there."

"I can get us there," said Calyssa. "And I don't know how I know, so don't ask."

"You want to take orders from a loony?" Thrash asked them. "Orders you don't even understand?"

"The jester's crazy," said Kellach, "but that's not why he's locked up. Either he knows something or he did something. Either way, following his directions should give us a little more information to work with. Right now, we're missing too many pieces of the puzzle. Unless you have a better idea about where to start searching."

Thrash scowled but said nothing.

Driskoll had Thrash tear a small piece of fabric from his sock. It might not be glamorous, but it should work for his spell. It was the only wool on hand, since the guards had taken Kellach's spell component pouch.

"I don't know about this, Dris," said Kellach. "If you get 'proon frabble' again, we're sunk."

"It's our only chance, Kellach. I'll get it right this time. Just don't jinx me." Singing barely above a whisper, Driskoll focused his concentration about twenty feet past their cell, where the corridor turned off to the left and right. As his tune drew to an end, he gestured with one hand.

From the intersection in the corridor came the sound of a cell door clanging open against a wall. It sounded exactly like their own cell door, except for a slight rising and lowering of the volume, a sort of thrumming effect. After a long pause, the sound repeated.

133

"Yes!" Driskoll's fists shot up in the air. "I did it! I told you I could do it." He looked back at Kellach.

"There's no time for celebrating, Dris," his brother answered. "Get back here!"

Driskoll crowded back with the others. They stood as if they were all still tied together. Calyssa grabbed the cords off the floor and hid in the back.

Within seconds, four guards hurried past to investigate the unexpected noises.

"Ah, it's probably just one of them banging their chains against their door," said one.

"You two go left," said another. "We'll check down this way."

As soon as they rounded the corner, Moyra threw herself into her work. In her hand was a tiny tool she had sewn into the hem of her shirt. "My dad taught me to always keep a backup," she'd explained when she removed it, "and this way, it never gets lost or stolen." Now she used it to pick the lock on their cell door. She moved deftly and silently, while Calyssa kept watch in case the guards returned. In almost no time they all heard the metal *clink* of success.

"Quick!" she whispered. She swung the door wide, stopping it before it hit the wall.

As the six of them scurried up the corridor toward the guard-room, they heard the jester hiss from behind them. "The dragons hold the power! Hurry!"

Moyra took the lead and signaled for them to stop a few feet shy of the guardroom doorway. She crept forward and peered in, then motioned for the others to follow her. They slipped into the empty guardroom.

"Let's grab our stuff quick and get out of here," she whispered.

"Where is it?" whispered Driskoll.

"You there!" a voice shouted behind them. "Halt!"

Two of the guards were running up the corridor toward them.

"Forget the stuff!" said Calyssa. "Run!"

They scrambled for the door leading out of the dungeons.

Just then, Lunk let out a yell. "Clobber!"

His mace was leaning against a cabinet in the far corner. His face lit up, and he strode across the guardroom.

The others stopped in their tracks, torn. None of them wanted to leave Lunk behind, but they had to run for their lives.

The two guards charged into the room. They looked at the unarmed kids at the other door, then at Lunk, going for his mace. Both leveled their spears at Lunk and closed in on him.

"Rrraaarrr!" Thrash let out a terrifying roar. Arms raised over his head, he stomped toward the guards.

The guards spun toward this unexpected threat.

Behind them, Lunk grabbed the backs of their collars and cracked their heads together with a loud *thunk*.

The guards dropped like stones.

While Lunk was reclaiming Clobber and collecting the guards' spears, Thrash tore open the cabinet door. Piled inside were the rest of their weapons and gear. "Hurry!" he said. He strapped on all of his many weapons in what had to be record time, then handed Lunk his things. "All this noise will bring the rest of the guard down on us."

The others followed Thrash's example. Calyssa grabbed several more spears from a rack on the wall.

More shouts rang out from the dungeon corridor. The other two guards had spotted the escaped prisoners and were racing toward them.

The fugitives fled through the guardroom door and into the corridor beyond.

"We can bar the door with these!" said Calyssa, holding out the spears.

Thrash helped her slide the shafts of the spears through the door handle. It wouldn't hold for long, but it might give them a head start.

With Thrash leading the way and Lunk bringing up the rear, they ran up the stone hallway to the first intersection.

"Which way?" asked Driskoll.

"To the main level." Calyssa pointed to the left. "That way."

They headed off in that direction, but Moyra hung back at the nearest torch. She pulled the bag of caltrops from her belt and scattered several of them on the floor behind her. Then she sprinted to catch up with the others, grabbing the torch from the wall as she went and leaving that section of corridor dark.

A violent *crack* from the direction of the dungeons told them the guards had broken out of the guardroom. In seconds, several angry voices rang out.

"They've called for reinforcements!" Thrash panted.

Driskoll groaned. "We need a place to hide!"

"There's no time!" Kellach said. "Come on!" He sprinted up another set of stairs, taking them two at a time.

Driskoll jogged up after his brother, breathing hard. Normally the little bit of running they'd done wouldn't bother him, but running while carrying all this gear wore him out fast.

Howls reached them from the halls below. The guards had found Moyra's caltrops.

"I knew those would come in handy," she said, sounding rather pleased with herself. "That should hold them for a little while."

"Let's go!" Calyssa said. "We're almost there."

They kept running, following Calyssa's directions as they went, down hallways and up stairways.

As they climbed to the top of yet another set of stairs, she turned to tell them in a hushed voice, "This is the main level. Look, the murals—"

"Wait!" said Driskoll, grabbing her arm. "Get down!"

They all ducked back down the stairs. The sounds of boots on stone thudded a quick but organized cadence from the direction Calyssa had been heading. The cadence reached a crescendo and came to a sudden halt.

"All right, you men," a voice barked. "This is where we split up. The previous watch captured several intruders, so keep an eye out. There could be others. You lot go that way. The rest of you, come with me. Now look alive."

Shouts went up from dozens of throats. "Sir! Yes, sir!" The clomping rhythm resumed and faded in two directions.

"How are we ever going to get past all those guards?" asked Moyra.

"We're not. See that mural?" Kellach pointed to the wall across from the landing. The elaborate artwork depicted a courtly scene. "The jester said, 'Follow the leader. The walls tell all.' The king in that painting is facing the direction those guards just came from. The king is the leader, right? I think we should go the way he's facing. And since the guards just came from there, they won't be going back there for a while."

The silence that greeted his suggestion made it plain that the others had little confidence in it.

Thrash muttered darkly under his breath, then motioned for Kellach to lead the way. "Let's just get moving," he said. "We're sitting ducks here."

They moved down the hallway with Kellach taking the lead. The scenes in the murals continued along the walls, depicting different parts of some tale none of them recognized.

The tale covered ages of Mios's mythology or history, probably a little of both, but the rulers—sometimes kings, sometimes queens—always bore the same crown, same robes, and same scepter with snarling dragons on top. And the rulers always faced the same direction.

"Those dragons on the scepter," Kellach murmured. "That must be what the jester was talking about when he said, 'The dragons hold the power.' See the rays of light streaming from the dragons? The scepter is a symbol of the leader's power. I think we're on the right track."

Every time the little group passed a doorway or an intersection, they expected to be discovered. Yet there seemed to be no one around. Perhaps the residents of this castle were keeping to their rooms for fear of more intruders. Or perhaps things had gone so horribly wrong in Mios that everyone except the guards had been thrown in the dungeons.

As they ran, Driskoll caught glimpses of rich tapestries, ornaments trimmed in gold, and countless works of art in the rooms lining the corridor. But no people. The emptiness gave the bright and beautiful place a haunted, sinister feeling. They were almost relieved to hear a voice coming from around the corner up ahead.

"All right. Now that they've had time to worry about what the Breaker will do to them, let's see if they've had any second thoughts."

It was the last voice they wanted to hear.

CHAPTER

20

"Captain Kruiq!" Kellach hissed.

"Quick!" said Calyssa, waving them through the nearest doorway. "In here."

They ducked into the room. Shelves of leather-bound books lined the walls from floor to ceiling. The six escapees flattened themselves against the shelves on either side of the doorway and listened.

"If they still won't talk," the captain continued from the hallway, "we're to bring them before him. We must absolutely ensure that this little audience goes smoothly."

"Yes, sir," came the reply. "I'll see to it personally. As soon as . . ."

The heavy tread of the two men muffled the rest of their exchange as they strode briskly past the room and moved on.

Moyra waited till the voices had faded completely before she peered out to make sure the coast was clear once more.

"That was close," she said as she came back in.

"Too close," said Thrash. "And it's about to get much closer.

Any second now, one of the guards is going to find the captain and tell him we've escaped. Once he raises the general alarm, there'll be no hiding place for us."

"Hiding place . . . " said Calyssa. "Wait. There's a hiding place somewhere in this room. It's . . . No, it's a secret passage! That's right. This whole place is riddled with them."

She held up the Eye, dangling it from its beads. "Show me where the murals lead."

Within the Eye, an image formed. It revealed a large, paneled room ringed with paintings. Then the Eye went dark.

"Yes, I remember that now," said Calyssa. "That's the Royal Gallery. It leads to the throne room."

She spoke to the Eye once more. "Show me the secret passage that leads to the Royal Gallery."

A blinding white light blazed from the Eye, streaming toward one set of shelves. Again the Eye went dark.

"Yes," she said, letting the Eye fall to the end of its chain once more. "I knew it was here somewhere. Come on. It'll be safer if we go this way."

She led them to the wall the Eye had pointed out and scanned the shelves. When she found the book she was looking for, she pressed it against the wall behind it.

They heard a click and a faint sliding sound. A small section of the shelves swung away from them, revealing a narrow corridor.

"Last one in, swing that shut behind you," she said.

As they followed her through the tight path, Moyra said, "That was a pretty lucky break, the way we happened to duck into a room that just happened to have a secret passage, and you just happened to remember it. It's almost too good to believe, don't you think?"

"I can't believe after all we've been through, you still don't trust me," she replied, rounding a corner.

"If you still don't remember who you are," said Moyra, "what makes you so sure I should trust you? Maybe you're one of the bad guys, and you just forgot."

Calyssa stopped. After a moment she said, "How do you know it's not the good guys that want you in the dungeons?" With that, she pushed on a section of wall and peeked through the narrow opening. Then she opened the section wider and stepped out of the secret passage.

The others exchanged uncomfortable glances, then followed her out. They found themselves in a long room with wood paneling. Double doors with ornate handles of gold stood closed at each end.

"This is the gallery," Calyssa told them. A faraway look clouded her eyes as she scanned the room. She pointed to one set of doors. "The throne room is through there. I'm not sure if the jester meant for us to come in here or go in there."

On the walls hung dozens of portraits in gilt frames. Each bore a gold plaque with a name inscribed in it.

"Prince Glimmindar. Queen Wayryn," Kellach read aloud as he walked along the nearest wall. "These must all be rulers of Mios."

"Yes," said Calyssa, crossing toward the far corner. "I think the ones closest to the throne room doors are the most recent. King Zoch. King Fonkin. Princess Aria." She gestured toward portraits here and there as she read the names below them.

Moyra trailed along after her and placed her ear to the door. After a still, tense moment, she shook her head. "I don't hear a thing."

She moved to where Calyssa stood staring at the last portrait. "Hey, look at this." There was an urgency in Moyra's voice that quickly brought the others huddling around.

"She's wearing a torque like yours," she said, pointing at the portrait of Princess Aria.

Calyssa raised her wrist to compare her bracelet to the one in the portrait. Both torques had twisted gold bands, with dragons facing each other. "Hm. They are a lot alike. But the dragons on hers are more like the portal dragon, crouching and snarling, not rampant like the ones on mine. And hers aren't holding a crystal."

"Maybe you're a long-lost cousin or something," said Moyra. She looked at the princess, with her pale hair and brownish-gray skin and her icy blue eyes. Then she looked at Calyssa's black ponytail and fair skin and her . . . icy blue eyes? Moyra looked at the portrait again. "Your eyes are exactly like hers."

"Maybe, but there's a slight problem with that theory," said Calyssa. "Under all that white hair, she has pointy ears. We're not even the same race. But I definitely know her from somewhere. She's the girl I remembered, the one I told you about. The one who's in danger."

"Maybe you were a lady-in-waiting," Driskoll suggested.

"Or her servant," said Kellach. "Maybe you witnessed what happened to her, something terrible. I've heard a really horrible experience can cause memory loss."

"Well, let's find this missing heir, so we can get out of here."

Thrash crossed the room and grasped the door handle. "I don't see anything here that will help us. I say we try the throne room."

Calyssa nodded, and they all moved in behind the half-orc.

Thrash pushed the left door open just a hair and peered through the crack. "All clear," he said, swinging the door wide.

The throne room was not much larger than the gallery, yet it was far more impressive. From the alabaster floor to the crystal chandeliers sparkling with the light of a million tiny suns, this room reflected the glory of the royalty. The six companions moved slowly into the room, as if trespassing on hallowed ground.

The walls were adorned with jewel-encrusted weapons, as well as a variety of heraldic crests and other ornaments fit for royalty. The throne itself dominated the far side of the room, the royal scepter leaning casually against the back of the chair. Near it stood a crystal statue of Zhigani.

"Wow," said Moyra. "Zhigani must really be a big shot in Mios. She's the only one honored with a statue in the throne room."

The statue faced the throne. The artist had rendered the fortune-teller with her arms outstretched, as if to receive an honor.

"What a strange spot for it, though," Driskoll remarked as they moved into the room. "It seems out of place."

"That's because it was just delivered," said a voice from the doorway.

The fugitives jumped and whirled in that direction. A tall man—by their current standards—in flowing robes of deep

144

violet paused on the threshold. His sharply arched eyebrows and straight beard edge gave him an intelligent but stern air.

"Who are you?" Thrash demanded.

The man walked toward them. He flashed them a cool smile. "I am Dur. And the statue that you were just commenting on was newly commissioned to honor Mios's faithful servant, Zhigani." Dur hung his head. "I'm afraid she was recently murdered."

"Murdered!" Calyssa gasped. She turned to her companions, as if hoping they had heard something different.

The others stood, stunned.

"Who could do such a thing?" she asked.

"We have not yet caught the villain," Dur replied. "I'm not at liberty to tell you anything more at this time."

"Amazing." Kellach gasped as he wandered toward the statue. "We saw her only yesterday. Your artisans must truly be masters, to have created such a fine sculpture in so little time. It doesn't seem possible." He had reached the front of the statue and was staring at the fortune-teller's face.

Dur gave a dismissive wave of his hand. "It's a complicated process. There's no time to go into all that now. There's a killer on the loose. Perhaps you can be of assistance to us in catching the fiend."

He walked slowly, thoughtfully, across the room. His robes swirled regally around him. "You say you saw her yesterday. You must tell me everything she told you. It may shed some light on this terrible crime."

Calyssa took a deep breath. "Well, first she—"

"—talked to me," Kellach interrupted. "Back in ValSages. I wanted her to tell my fortune. My five friends here were all sure

145

she was a phony, so the five of them went to buy dragon's draft while Zhigani read my palm."

The others looked at him sharply. They all knew he was lying, but they didn't know why. They also knew he wouldn't do so without good reason, so they kept quiet.

"So she read your palm," said Dur. He moved closer to the throne. "Then what?"

Kellach shrugged, backing away from the statue a few steps. "Not much, really. Let's see. She asked for our help and told us to meet her near here. Then she never showed up. We went looking for her and got lost. That's when the guards grabbed us and threw us in the dungeons."

"I see." The man laid a hand on the armrest of the throne while he considered this. "And how did you know how to open the portal?"

"What?" said Kellach. "Oh. Uh, like I said, Zhigani told us how, back in ValSages."

"You never said that."

A bead of sweat appeared at Kellach's temple. "Didn't I? I thought I mentioned it."

"Of course," said Dur. "So tell me, what was it she wanted you to help her with?"

"Um, she needed help finding someone," he hedged. "She wasn't specific. She said she'd give us all the details when we got to the meeting place."

"I see," said Dur. "Any idea why she would ask you for help? Why not the city guardsmen? Or some other adults?"

"Because where we come from, the guardsmen and other adults are all too busy to go off helping strangers. Kids like us, on the other hand, are always looking for new and interesting things to do. Especially when there's a chance we'll get rich in the process."

"She offered to pay you?"

"No, not directly," said Kellach, "but when she read my palm, she said she saw some sort of treasure in store for me. I just figured . . . Well, it seems foolish now, of course. Anyway, that's all I can remember her telling us. Does that help you at all?"

Dur smiled that same cold smile. "I think it might. Thank you. I feel it's safe now to tell you that Zhigani went looking for help on my orders. So in a way, you've been working for me all along. And now that she's no longer with us, I need your help more than ever. You see, she was trying to find my heir, Princess Aria. The princess was kidnapped, and I can't tell you how grateful I would be if the legendary Knights of the Silver Dragon would aid me in my quest for her safe return." He turned and seated himself on the throne.

"Kidnapped," Calyssa breathed. She spoke as if talking in her sleep.

"Wait a minute," said Thrash. "Your heir? You're saying you're the king? But the jester said the king was dead."

Kellach gave him a dirty look.

"The jester? The one in the dungeons?" said Dur. He shook his head sadly. "He is quite mad, you know. Dangerously so. You mustn't believe anything he says. I am the ruler here. And as you can see, King Dur is very much alive indeed."

"Yeah? Okay," said Thrash, his tone belligerent. "Then why did you have us thrown in the dungeons if you wanted our help?"

Kellach glared at Thrash.

"Oh, I am sorry about that," said King Dur. "That was all just a terrible misunderstanding."

Thrash scowled. "What do you mean, a—"

"Well, thank goodness that's all it was," Kellach interrupted. "Because now I feel it's safe to tell you that we have, in fact, returned Princess Aria to you."

The king's eyes lit up and locked on him, much like a serpent locking onto a mouse. "You have? Where is she?"

Kellach gestured grandly toward Calyssa. "There she is, standing right in front of you."

CHAPTER

21

Everyone, including Calyssa herself, simply stood gaping at Kellach.

"It's true," he insisted. "See that torque on her wrist? See how much it looks like the one in the portrait of Princess Aria? Take the crystal out of yours, Calyssa."

Calyssa eyed Kellach suspiciously, as if she suspected all the excitement and fear might have driven him quite mad. Gingerly she grasped the silver crystal and removed it from between the two dragons.

In the pause between one breath and the next, Calyssa's black ponytail turned white, her fair skin became brownish-gray, and her slightly elven face took on the smaller, broader features of a gnome. The dragons on the torque revealed their true form as well: snarling, not rampant. Only the slaver's brand on her arm remained to show that Calyssa and Princess Aria were one and the same.

Calyssa gazed at the wide-eyed faces around her. Though her recent adventures had left her somewhat grimy and tattered, it was plain that she really was the princess, all the way down to her pointy ears.

"Fluffy?" Lunk whispered. His voice sounded small and plaintive in the large room.

"Princess Aria!" Dur gasped. He jumped to his feet and stood staring at her. His eyes bulged.

Calyssa touched her face and her ears, slowly taking in her changed form. "How . . . how did you know?" she asked Kellach.

"It was a lot of things, really. But mostly it was what the jester said: 'The dragons hold the power.' I realized the dragons on your torque were holding back your true form."

Dur's mouth opened and shut, but no words came out. He looked like a fish gasping for water. The smile he finally managed to scrape onto his face looked like it had been nailed there.

"Now, I believe King Dur is overcome with relief by your return, *Fluffy*," said Kellach. "Hey, *Fluffy*, I mean, Calyssa. Why don't you give him a nice, warm greeting like the one you gave Thrash when you two first met?"

The princess glanced at Kellach from the corner of her eye. Though her appearance had changed entirely, her gestures and mannerisms remained the same.

She slipped the crystal into her pocket and glided toward King Dur, arms thrown wide as if to embrace him. When she reached him, she clasped his shoulders. Her foot swung back, up, above her shoulder. *Whap!*

Dur cried out in pain, and his hands flew to his nose. Too late. He staggered back, his eyes watering and blood flowing from beneath his fingers.

Kellach began casting a spell under his breath. As he finished his incantation, he pointed at the royal scepter leaning against the throne just beyond Zhigani's outstretched hands. The staff flashed across the room.

The princess snatched the scepter from the air. At the top of the scepter two snarling dragons faced each other, just like the ones on her torque. Brandishing it like a quarterstaff, she held it with a white-knuckle grip between herself and the man who called himself the king.

"I don't understand," said Dur. He looked into his bloody hands as if they might hold the answers he sought. When they did not, he lifted his gaze to Calyssa. "What is the meaning of this?"

Kellach moved cautiously toward them. "The portraits showed important information that revealed who Princess Aria was, but just as important is what they did not show." He paused, watching Calyssa. "They did not show King Dur. All the royalty of Mios is immortalized on those walls, even down to the missing heir. But no King Dur. Why? Because you are no king."

"Not only that," Kellach went on, "but you also mentioned that we're Knights of the Silver Dragon. We didn't tell you that, so there are only two ways you could have gotten that information. One, from the man in the pit, the one who tried to kill us all. Or two, from Zhigani herself, which would mean you lied about her death. And I know that you did, because she's not dead. She's right there!"

Pointing at the fortune-teller's crystal form, he told his friends, "That's no statue. That really is Zhigani! And if you lied about Zhigani, you probably had a hand in turning her into a statue. For that alone, you deserve at least a bloody nose."

Dur laughed, dabbing his sleeve to his nose to stanch the flow of blood. "Think you're pretty clever, don't you, little wizard? Well, perhaps you are. But not clever enough. You see, the princess still doesn't even remember who she is, much less how to unleash the power of the royal scepter."

Calyssa's eyes shifted nervously back and forth. "I . . . I . . . "

"She remembers," Kellach said. "She merely wants answers from you before she has you removed."

"Yes, answers." Calyssa squared her shoulders and rapped the scepter against the floor for emphasis.

"You think I don't know you're lying?" Dur laughed. "No matter. I'd like some answers too. Let's ask Captain Kruiq. This is all his fault anyway. His and that idiotic alchemist's. If they'd just killed you like I told them to, there'd have been no problem."

"You told them to kill me?" Calyssa said softly. "Why?"

"Power, of course!" Dur snarled. He shook with rage. A mad fury gleamed from his eyes. "That old fool Fonkin got to rule for years!"

"Fonkin?" said Driskoll. "Who's Fonkin?"

Dur scowled. "King Fonkin, my brother, the last ruler of Mios. He was as naïve and weak as his heir." Dur gestured to Calyssa.

Calyssa frowned. "My . . . father?"

"Yes," said Dur. "When he died, you were too young to assume the throne. So it fell to your dear Uncle Dur to run things until you came of age."

CHAPTER

22

Calyssa set her crystal between the two dragons atop the scepter. White light flared out from it like a sunburst, surrounding the princess in a sphere of radiance. The glowing orb expanded to shield her friends, catching the infinite rays of silver from Dur's wand and the chandeliers and drawing them into the scepter. The crystal atop the scepter absorbed the silver rays, filtered them, and released them in a stream of blinding white light.

Raw power roared through the room as the two opposing magics fed upon each other, escalating. The ornaments rattled on the walls, and the chandeliers rang as they shook.

The stream of blinding light swallowed Dur and Kruiq. Encased within that brilliance, they looked as if they were made of light. The wand shook in Dur's hand, but still the silver rays flowed from it.

Kellach took a few items from his pouch. His hand traced a complex design in the air as he finished.

"Get that wand!" he shouted.

Driskoll stared at his brother. Who was he shouting at? Was he crazy? There was no way for any of them to get the wand without being crystallized or destroyed. Maybe both.

The wand was suddenly plucked from Dur's motionless hand as if by some invisible force. It simply floated before him, just out of his reach.

All fell still.

The silver downpour came to an abrupt halt. Only the white light from the scepter remained. The sudden stillness that fell over the room felt like the end of time. For several ragged breaths, no one dared to move.

Calyssa stood before the throne, white light fading around her like mist burning off a lake at sunrise. Dur stood exactly as he had before, wrapped in light, as if frozen in time. In the doorway was the light-encased form of Captain Kruiq.

Thrash broke the silence. "What happened?"

"It looks like the princess got her memories back," Kellach said.

Calyssa smiled shyly. "Well, not all of them, but I did remember how to use the scepter. It needed the crystal to work." She pointed at the crystal now stuck between the two dragons at the top of the scepter. "It's funny, in a way. If Dur hadn't brought up my father, I wouldn't have remembered in time. But he is the one who taught me how to use the scepter."

"Oh, yeah," said Thrash with a forced laugh. "Real funny."

The others laughed too, the tension beginning to lift.

Driskoll turned to his brother. "How did you get Dur's wand?"

"I cast a spell to create an invisible servant and ordered it take Dur's wand," Kellach explained.

Thrash's jaw dropped. "Well, why didn't you do that before?" he sputtered.

"It wouldn't have worked. The invisible servant couldn't have forced Dur to release the wand, but Dur couldn't resist it while he was . . . whatever you call that." He gestured vaguely to Dur's light-covered form.

"Give the wand to the princess," Kellach told his invisible helper. The wand drifted over and slipped into Calyssa's hand.

"What do we do now?" asked Driskoll.

"First I want to summon the guards. We'll need their help with these traitors." She stepped over to the throne and touched a crystal that was set into one of the armrests.

"Um, Fluffy?" said Thrash quietly. "I mean, Your Princess-ship?" He frowned at the floor and shuffled his feet awkwardly.

"Actually, it's 'Your Highness,'" she said with a grin, "but in your case, I'll settle for Calyssa. And don't worry. Your cousin is next."

She walked over to Lunk's crystallized form and pointed the crystal wand at him. The wand flashed silver, and a beam of silver light shot from it to engulf Lunk. When the light dissipated, the half-orc emerged, his true form restored.

"Rrrrr!" The roar he began when he'd launched himself at Dur continued now, and Lunk advanced a few more steps before he realized his enemy was frozen and no longer holding the wand.

He looked at the scene around him, puzzled. His gaze settled on the princess, who had mysteriously replaced the girl with the black ponytail. "Fluffy?"

"That's right, big fellah."

The big half-orc looked unconvinced.

"See?" The princess held up the Eye of Fortune. "Big magic."

"Fluffy!" His face split into a broad grin.

Thrash went over and clapped his cousin on the shoulder. "Good to have you back, buddy."

Then the princess turned to Zhigani's crystallized form. "We'll need her help sorting this all out."

"By the way," Driskoll asked Kellach, "how did you know this was Zhigani and not just a crystal statue?"

"It's hard to explain," said Kellach, suppressing a grin. "You have to look at things from my perspective."

He pointed at Zhigani's face.

Rendered in crystal perfection on the left side of Zhigani's face was an eye patch, and on that eye patch, rendered in the same crystal perfection were the words "Only in ValSages."

Driskoll and Calyssa laughed.

The others crowded around to see what was so funny. Soon they were all snickering and shaking their heads in disbelief.

Calyssa used the wand on Zhigani. The seeress, returned to her true form, continued her lunge for the scepter. Only it wasn't there anymore. She whirled, ready to fight. Surprise dawned on her face as she took in the condition of Dur, Kruiq, and the room full of kids.

"Your Highness!" she exclaimed. "You're safe! And you're . . . you again!"

Calyssa smiled fondly. "Yes, my friend. Thanks to you and a few well-chosen allies." She quickly introduced her to the others.

"As you can see, we still have some unfinished business." She nodded toward Dur and Kruiq. "But there's still so much we don't know. Like how many people were in on this plot. We've caught these two, and one is dead. How many more are still out there?"

"I don't know," Zhigani said. "The Eye showed me someone trying to kill you. Unfortunately, as is often the case with divination, many important details were missing."

"Speaking of the Eye, you should have it back now." The princess took the Eye of Fortune from her necklace and handed it to the old woman.

"Oh, thank you," said Zhigani, taking off the silly eye patch and putting the Eye back where it belonged. "I've felt so lost without it."

"I know how to find out about our enemies," Calyssa added. "Watch this."

She aimed the scepter at Captain Kruiq's light-encased form in the doorway. White light streamed over him, releasing him.

The captain ran into the throne room. "The prisoners have escaped!" He pulled up short, his uncomprehending gaze shifting from the fugitives to the light-enveloped form of Dur to the princess.

His jaw dropped, and he turned to run.

The crystal atop the scepter winked to silver, and white light streamed from it to the retreating captain. Bands of white energy wrapped themselves around his struggling form, stopping him in his tracks.

"That's a handy little gadget," said Kellach. "I don't suppose you have a few more like it lying around?"

Calyssa threw him a brash smile. "Hey, I deserve something for putting up with all this royalty stuff. Don't I?" Then she was all business again, using the scepter to draw the captain back to her, his heels dragging across the throne room floor.

"Captain Kruiq," she said. "You have some explaining to do."

The captain squirmed, but the magical bonds held him fast. "It wasn't my fault!" he declared. "This was all Dur's doing."

The princess clucked her tongue. "Captain, I'm disappointed in you. You were sworn to defend us. And now you dishonor yourself further with lies? It is a sad day for Mios indeed. You see, Dur told us you were behind the whole thing."

"That's a lie!" Kruiq bellowed.

Calyssa sighed. "I hate to do this, but you leave me no choice. I will have to invoke the Talons of Truth."

A rope of energy branched off from the radiance encircling the captain, drawing itself into the form of a giant claw that hovered in front of him. The talons of light appeared undeniably lethal.

"You will tell us what you know of the plot against me," the princess said flatly. "If you utter a single falsehood, the talons will tear out your heart. Speak."

The captain's eyes went wide. "I . . . I . . . "

A single talon of light gently but impatiently tapped the center of the man's chest. "Do not waste my time!" snapped the princess. "How many of you were there behind this plot?"

"Three of us, Your Highness," the captain stammered. His eyes remained fixed on the claw, and he winced as he spoke. "Lord Dur, Namnock, and myself."

"Tell us about this Namnock."

"He is—was—an alchemist, Your Highness. A former guard who dishonored himself and was cast out. Dur needed him to concoct the poison to kill you so he could rule in your stead. I put the poison in your food, but Namnock fouled up the mixture. Instead of killing you, it only clouded your memories."

Calyssa's eyes narrowed to angry slits. "Then what happened?"

"Dur ordered us to finish you off, but you escaped. Since it was Namnock's fault, I had him follow the seeress. I knew she'd lead us to you. But that dolt Namnock was gone so long, I decided to go find out what was going on. Turns out he had lost her and had come up with some scheme to get these surface-dwellers to tell him where you were hiding. I figured a former guard who couldn't even tail one old woman was completely useless. So I did away with him and followed the seeress myself, but she came back here instead of leading me to you."

The princess said nothing for a moment. Sadness and pain filled her eyes.

"Why?" she asked at last.

"Why, Your Highness?"

"Why would you all plot to take my life?"

Kruiq looked puzzled. "Riches, of course, power, prestige . . . All the things you have that we didn't."

The princess rasped between clenched teeth, "You tried to take my life because you were greedy? Not for some grand cause or ideal you believed in? Not for some political disagreement or even some personal grievance? Just blind, stupid selfishness?"

Kruiq seemed to shrink within the grip of the scepter's energy.

At that moment, a small group of guards trooped through the gallery and into the throne room.

"There're the fugitives!" shouted Lieutenant Flim. "And they've got the captain! Seize them!"

CHAPTER

23

"Oh, stop that," said Calyssa. She waved the scepter at the guards, and white light flared out from it. Suddenly their uniforms all turned to frilly dresses, and their weapons became lollipops. "Or must I bind you like Kruiq?"

Their surprise at the princess's return turned to alarm when they realized she had taken their commanding officer into custody. Flim looked uncertain as to whether he should curtsy or salute. He settled for dropping to one knee, and the others followed his example.

"Forgive us, Your Highness," said Flim. "We were under orders. We didn't know . . . "

"Disregard any orders you received during my absence. We will talk in more detail later. Lock Kruiq and Dur in the dungeons." She waved the scepter again, returning the guards' uniforms and weapons, then she turned it on Dur. His cocoon of light dissolved and turned to bands like those holding Kruiq.

"And free the jester," she added. "See that he's cared for."

As the guards tied up Dur and Kruiq, Calyssa said, "I weep for my realm, that it produced traitors like you." Then she turned her back on them.

Dur glared, plots for revenge already smoldering in his eyes. Kruiq merely stood, head bowed in shame and defeat, until the guards led them away.

When they were gone, Zhigani chuckled. "Nice touch," she told the princess. "Talons of Truth. Ha!"

Calyssa blushed. "I just made that up to get him to talk," she confessed to the others. "He could have claimed to be a goat turning cartwheels, and the scepter wouldn't have known the difference."

"There's something else I'm still wondering about, though," Calyssa said to Zhigani. "How did we manage to escape?"

"Well, when I foresaw the plot against you, I ran to your side, hoping to get you to safety until I could get more information. I was nearly too late. The potion had made you groggy and confused, and I knew we didn't have much time. I stole the royal crystal and placed it in your torque to magically disguise you. Then I used a Dragon's Eye—"

"Ah! I'd forgotten about those," the princess interrupted. She turned to the others to explain. "A Dragon's Eye is a rare crystal that creates a one-time, one-person portal. The crystal is destroyed in the process, so they're only used in the gravest emergencies."

Zhigani continued. "I couldn't just hide you here in Mios, because I didn't know who to trust. So I consulted the Eye. It foresaw that we would secure the help of Mios's ancient allies, the Knights of the Silver Dragon, in a place called ValSages."

"Wait a minute," said Driskoll. "How did the Knights and the people of Mios become allies? How did they even know about each other?"

"Ah, that's a very long story," the seeress said with a twinkle in her eye. "A long story for another time. I'll let Zendric decide when you're ready for that.

"Now as I was saying, the Eye showed me an image of Val-Sages. I knew my mere presence would give away Princess Aria's identity, magical disguise or not, so I created a portal to ValSages and pushed her through it."

The princess looked hurt. "I'll have you know, the game hall slavers found me alone and with no memories, so they just snatched me up and told me I was a slave. And I believed them!"

"I'm sorry, Your Highness," said Zhigani. "But your life and your throne depended on it. What else could I have done?"

"Well, under the circumstances . . . " said Calyssa.

"Exactly," said the seeress. She continued her explanation. "Once you were gone, I went through the common portal. That's the one all of you came through," she added to the others.

"Namnock followed me, though I didn't know that at the time. I sneaked off to ValSages, and the Eye showed me where to wait. I posed as a fortune-teller while searching for the princess and the Knights, and watching out for enemies. That's when you came in," she said to Kellach, Driskoll, and Moyra.

"Needless to say, you weren't exactly the Knights I was expecting," she went on. "I was certain there'd been some mistake. So I showed you the image of a treasure chest to get rid of you, but for some reason the Eye showed the image of the

165

princess in her disguise. I'd swear the thing turns enigmatic just to get attention sometimes."

She shook her head. "I should have trusted it, but I remained convinced you couldn't help us. When I located Princess Aria, I arranged to meet her in the catacombs. I had planned to return to Mios, where I could help her use the scepter to regain her memories and reclaim her throne.

"On the way there, I discovered Namnock tailing me. I didn't know who he was, but I knew he would follow me to get to her. So I led him off into the paths and lost him. In the time it took to do that, I missed meeting the princess. So I decided to tail him, to find out who our enemies were and what they were planning. He went back to the pit, and that's where Kruiq caught up with him. I heard Namnock tell Kruiq that he had set you up to fall into the trap."

She nodded toward Driskoll. "He saw you talking to me and recognized your pin. That's when I finally realized you Knights had a part to play in all this, children or not. So after Kruiq killed Namnock, I let him spot me, and I led him away from the pit to keep him from killing you. In the end, though, Dur caught me. I failed. I'm sorry, Your Highness. I should have been able to protect you better."

"Nonsense," said the princess. "With little information and less time, you still managed to save the day. Just because you received help from some unexpected sources doesn't mean you failed. After all, Dur's plans would have succeeded if not for you. Not bad for a mere seeress."

Zhigani smiled. "Not bad, yourself," she said.

"I just remembered something else," Calyssa added. "We've

166

hardly had anything to eat all day. I'm starving! Let's go to the dining hall, and I'll have a feast prepared for all of us."

"Your Highness—" Kellach began.

"Please," she interrupted. "It's just us here. Call me Aria."

"We've called you so many things, it's hard to keep track," he joked. "We'd love to stay, but we've been gone a long time. Our parents will be worried sick."

"Of course," she replied. "I'll have something brought for you to eat on the way home. Zhigani and I can go with you as far as the portal, and I'll arrange an escort to see you safely back to your city." She led them through the gallery and out into the corridor beyond.

As they walked, it occurred to Driskoll how strange it seemed now to move about these halls without skulking and hiding. He marveled at how quickly things can change. Princess Aria, once the streetwise runaway Fluffy then the haunted and mysterious Calyssa, was now the self-assured ruler of a hidden realm. He wondered how much this adventure had changed the rest of them. He didn't feel different. Well, maybe a little.

When they arrived at the room with the portal, Lieutenant Flim had already informed the guards there of the heir's return. Princess Aria instructed him to make arrangements for food and prepare an escort for his former captives. With a deep bow, he hurried to obey.

"What will happen to Dur and Kruiq?" Kellach asked.

"I haven't figured that out yet," the princess admitted. "It might serve them right just to rot in the dungeons, but even that seems too good for them. I'm sure Zhigani will be happy to help me see to it that those traitors get what's coming to them."

Zhigani nodded emphatically. "Speaking of getting what one deserves," she said, "when I first saw that the Knights of the Silver Dragon were only children, I was sure there'd been some mistake. But you children amazed me. You succeeded in saving not only Princess Aria, but also myself and all Mios as well. Your heroism shall become one of the great legends of this realm."

Lunk's head jerked up, and his nose twitched. He'd been even more quiet than usual since Fluffy had turned into the princess. Now he said just one word, but he said it with great enthusiasm. "Chicken."

A door opened, and a servant entered with a tray of roasted chickens.

"You all like chicken, don't you?" Princess Aria asked.

In answer, Lunk grabbed two chickens and dug in immediately.

Everyone else just grinned.

"I can't wait to tell everyone back home about all that's happened to us," said Driskoll. "They're never going to believe it!"

"Ah, there's just one slight problem with that," said the princess. "You can't tell anyone."

Driskoll gaped at her, his dreams of fame and glory crushed before they'd really gotten rolling. "Can't tell them what? Which part can't I tell? Please don't say I can't tell the part about the dungeons!"

There was sympathy in Aria's eyes, but she made no compromise. "I'm sorry. You can't tell anyone anything about this. Except Zendric, of course. Mios has been cut off from the surface world for ages, and we intend to keep it that way. You see, the crystals here are so plentiful and so powerful that it would create utter turmoil in your world if they were suddenly available there."

Driskoll's shoulders slumped. "Great," he muttered. "I finally get my hands on an amazing story no one has ever heard before, and I can't tell it? I may have to find a new calling in life."

"Oh, quit whining," said Moyra. "We'll just go back to Val-Sages, where you're bound to get yourself into more trouble—something a little more conventional this time, please—and you'll have a brand new story."

He made a face at her. "Very funny."

The princess looked at each of them in turn. "Do I have your word that you will keep Mios and her crystals our little secret?"

They all nodded solemnly, except for Lunk, who was too busy with his feasting. Thrash elbowed him. "You promise too. Right, Lunk?"

"Right, Thrash," he smacked around a chicken leg.

"I don't know, Your Highness," said Zhigani. "I don't think he quite understands what we're asking of him."

"Don't worry," said Thrash. "No one would believe anything he said anyway. Everybody thinks he's completely stupid."

Satisfied, the princess gave a quick nod.

She leaned over to whisper to Zhigani.

The seeress gazed at her ruler for a long moment. Then she excused herself and slipped out of the room.

An awkward silence fell.

Kellach cleared his throat. "I hate to say this, but we should probably be going. They're bound to be looking for us by now."

The others reluctantly agreed.

"And I certainly have my work cut out for me here," said Aria. "Very well then. Lieutenant, return our friends to their natural size."

Flim hurried to fetch the sapphire wand. With trembling hands he touched the blue wand to each of the five surface-dwellers.

Driskoll grimaced. His skin felt like it was shrinking around him, growing too tight for him to wear. The Miosians appeared to be getting shorter, but he realized it was he who was growing taller.

For the first time, he looked down on Princess Aria, and that's when it hit him. She wasn't coming with them. A part of him had known this as soon as Kellach had revealed her true identity and she'd removed her magical disguise. But now it was painfully obvious that they didn't belong here, and she didn't belong with them. And they wouldn't be dropping in on each other any time soon either. A lump swelled in his throat. "I'll miss you," he blurted, surprising himself more than anyone.

The princess smiled fondly at him. "And I'll miss all of you," she replied. "But it gives me hope that we may not have to remain hidden forever, knowing there are such heroes as you in your world."

Just then, Zhigani returned with a delicate box covered in silver velvet. She opened it and held it out for the princess.

"You're sure?" the seeress asked.

The princess nodded.

"I have something I'd like to give to each of you," she told them.

CHAPTER

24

The kids exchanged curious glances. None of them had any idea what the princess was up to.

"I present these to you as a reward for your service to this realm, as my thanks for keeping its secrets, and also just to make sure you don't forget me." Aria laughed. "I forgot myself once, and it caused a great deal of trouble. I want to discourage that sort of thing."

The princess reached a slender hand into the velvet box and took out a round, black crystal. "This is a Dragon's Eye," she said, holding it up. It seemed to absorb light rather than reflect it. "I'm giving one to each of you."

Driskoll's jaw dropped. "To us? But didn't you say they're extremely rare?"

"Don't argue with the princess, runt," said Thrash. "She wants to give us a present. You don't want to insult her by not taking it, do you?"

Aria smiled. "Yes, Driskoll, the crystals are rare and growing rarer. But they are not so rare as friends like the five of you. Do not use them lightly, for there will be no more. But in time of direst need, do not hesitate to use them to come back to Mios, and I will give you whatever aid is in my power to give. It's my way of thanking all of you for helping me reclaim my throne and myself. I would never have made it without you, and that's one thing I shall never forget."

The five surface-dwellers silently accepted her gift. They didn't know what to say.

Lunk stared at his crystal, dwarfed by his beefy paw. He looked to Thrash.

"No, Lunk," his cousin answered before the big healer could ask. "It's not food. It's . . . big magic."

"Maybe you'd better hold onto his until you can explain it to him," Aria suggested.

Lunk reached over with one massive paw and patted her tiny head. "Nice, good Fluffy," he said.

Reluctantly, they said their good-byes. Then, one by one, the surface-dwellers stepped through the glowing portal.

Driskoll shuddered at the tingling sensation as he teleported to the cavern with the great stone dragon. Blinking to clear the silver spots from his vision, he started down the path to the base of the chamber.

Kellach and Moyra were walking in front of him. Thrash and Lunk came behind. Lieutenant Flim took the lead, and three guards brought up the rear, two of them carrying torches.

Driskoll looked over his shoulder at the glowing portal. The stone dragon's eye reappeared, sealing the path to Mios.

Across the chamber, the dim torchlight revealed the opening to the crystal paths, now black and jagged again. Flim located a hidden lever and pulled it. Clicks and rattles came from behind the lever and faded into the distance. The black crystal walls turned smooth and silver once more.

The Miosian escort led the band of adventurers quickly through the path, out to the pit.

When they reached the third door, Lieutenant Flim came to a stop. "We must take our leave of you here." He gestured down the tunnel. "At the end of this passageway, there is a black crystal tile set into the floor at a chasm's edge. If you step on that tile, you will find a staircase that will return you to your world."

Kellach grinned at Thrash. "Yes, yes, we know all about it."

"Thank you for returning our princess." Flim bowed and handed his torch to Kellach. All the guards raised their fists in farewell as the five kids slipped through the doorway and down the tunnel.

The vast cavern loomed before them, just as creepy as they remembered it. The bats had returned to their respective ceiling and cliff faces.

Through the gloom, Driskoll tried to make out the door on the other side of the chasm, but torchlight was no match for the Eye of Fortune. "Who wants to go first?" he asked in his quietest voice.

"I'll do it," said Thrash. "I've already tried it, sort of."

"Shouldn't we light some more torches?" asked Kellach. "How are we all going to see where we're going if we have to cross one at a time?"

"We won't need torches to get across," Thrash replied. "Watch."

Thrash stepped onto the tile. As his feet came together on

it, a new black tile appeared, floating just a step up and out from the chasm's edge.

He brought his other foot onto the tile. "See? Without torches, we can't really look down. It's actually easier this way."

The faint silver glow of the first tile gave just enough light to show the next one.

Thrash strode calmly up over the abyss, his small form growing even smaller as he moved away.

Just when Driskoll thought he could bear the silent wait no longer, the black tile marked "To Promise" reappeared at the chasm's edge.

Kellach said, "After you, little brother."

Driskoll started to protest.

"What's the matter?" said Kellach. "Scared?"

The younger brother shot him a look. He was tempted to argue with Kellach, but he'd probably lose anyway. Besides, he wanted to get home. "Are you kidding?" he fired back. "This whole adventure was my idea. Remember?"

He stepped up to the edge of the void and gazed out over it. An updraft tugged at his shirttail. "'To Promise'," he said, reading the silver lettering of the tile aloud.

"Don't look down," said Moyra.

So naturally, Driskoll looked down. A queasy feeling washed over him. "Do me a favor, will you?" he told her. "Don't help."

"Sorry," she mumbled.

He forced his gaze upward and set first one foot onto the black tile, then the other. He expected it to wobble or sway, like a tiny raft on an ocean of air. Instead, it felt amazingly solid, just as if he were standing on a perfectly ordinary stair.

The next tile appeared in front of him. He swallowed hard and stepped up onto it.

He risked a glance back at his brother, standing at the edge of the abyss. "See you on the other side," he said with a weak effort at a smile.

His brother nodded and raised a hand in salute.

Driskoll stepped up onto the next step, then the next. He realized Thrash was right. This was easier with only the light of the tiles.

When at last he reached the door in the cliff face, he wanted to shout with relief. As he took the last step up to the sheer cliff wall, the door swung silently outward, providing a glimpse of a lighter shade of black. He hesitated, peering suspiciously through the opening. The door opened into the bottom of a wooded ravine, lost in shadows under the night sky. With one foot on the last tile and one foot on the ground, Driskoll paused for one final look back.

All he saw was the relentless black of the cavern below.

He moved ahead, and the door swung shut behind him. He drew in a deep breath of the clear, moist air. The night was almost black, with only a sliver of moon to hint at the shapes around him. He found himself surrounded by forest. Zhigani had told them they would come out less than half a mile northeast of the main gate to the ruins, but from what he could see, they might be miles from anywhere.

He turned to find the door had completely vanished. It had to be built into the side of the ravine itself, but there was certainly no sign of it now. Driskoll doubted it would be any more visible in broad daylight.

When Kellach, Moyra, and Lunk had joined Thrash and Driskoll in the ravine, they all set out for the road leading from the ruins back to the main highway. Before long, they saw the lights of several torches ahead.

"From the direction they're moving," said Moyra, "I'd say it's a party from Curston heading into the ruins."

"What, at night?" said Driskoll. "Who'd be that crazy?"

"Only a search party," Kellach replied with a sigh.

The kids approached cautiously, in case they'd stumbled upon a less friendly group. But sure enough, a large search party from Curston had come looking for them.

"Oh, we're in for it now," said Driskoll.

"Maybe we should split up here, then," said Thrash. "If your dad remembers me from our last run-in, we'll all have way too much explaining to do."

Before the others could answer, a bone-chilling howl split the night air. A second answered it, then a third.

"Uh-oh," said Kellach.

"Sounds like you've been hanging around him too long," said Thrash, hooking his thumb at Lunk.

A smile briefly touched Kellach's lips at that. "No, but the search party brought hounds with them. Too late to split up now."

The hounds intercepted them, baying madly. Uncertain what the dogs had found, the search party followed cautiously. Leading them, of course, was . . .

"Dad!" Driskoll ran and threw his arms around his father.

"Driskoll! Kellach!" Torin grabbed each of his boys by the shoulders, as if to convince himself they were real. "Are you all right?"

"We're fine," said Kellach. "How did you know where to find us?"

"Call it a hunch," Torin replied with a meaningful scowl. "I mean, just because you boys keep coming back here, even though I've told you it is absolutely not allowed, why would I expect to find you here? Tell me, what's it going to take to keep you away from here? What punishment haven't we tried yet? What were you thinking, coming out here again?"

The boys glanced nervously at their companions. "Uh, we . . . ," Driskoll began lamely.

Torin followed their gazes. He nodded a quick greeting to Moyra. "Who are these other two?"

"Friends," Driskoll blurted, surprised to realize that much was true. "They're our friends."

"They were helping me," Thrash spoke up. "That's what they were doing out here."

Torin favored him with a hard stare. "Helping you do what, exactly?"

"Find my cousin. He wandered off again," said Thrash. He elbowed Lunk in the ribs. "Tell the nice man where you went, Lunk."

"Went with Fluffy," said Lunk.

"He goes off chasing bunny rabbits sometimes," Thrash improvised, tapping his finger to his temple. "Calls them all Fluffy. He doesn't know any better. So these three helped me find him and bring him back. That's all."

"That's all, eh?" Torin looked at each of them in the flickering torchlight, obviously unconvinced. Then he peered at Thrash and Lunk. "You look familiar. Where have I seen you before?"

The big warrior hesitated.

"He looks just like that famous bard," Driskoll chimed in. "Doesn't he?"

"What famous bard?"

"Oh, Dad, you know the one," said Driskoll. "He sings that song, the one that goes:

Loony, loony Jester!
An avalanche for brains!
The goose has people-pimples,
And no princess remains! "

"What kind of cracked song is that?" asked Torin.

"Just ignore him, Dad," said Kellach. "We're all safe. So no harm done."

"No harm done," said Torin, "except for all these men out here risking their necks looking for you, and fewer watchers patrolling the town because of this, and me . . . "

Torin ranted on as he marched them all back to town. When they got inside the city gates, he ordered one of the watchers to take Moyra home and another to accompany the half-orcs.

"Take care, you two," said Driskoll as the half-orcs headed off.

"You too," said Thrash. "And stay clear of men selling maps."

As they watched the half-orcs walk away, Torin asked, "What did he mean by that?"

"It's just an expression, Dad," said Kellach. "Like, 'Don't take any lead coins'."

Torin shook his head. "You kids come up with the strangest sayings," he sighed. "Now, about your punishment . . . "

As they headed for home, Driskoll put his hand in his pocket. His fingers closed around the Dragon's Eye from Princess Aria, and a grin tugged at the corner of his mouth. Maybe the Dragon's Eye didn't come in a treasure chest, but the comfort of having an emergency portal in his pocket was definitely worth a fortune.

Now if he could just get that jester's song out of his head.

Acknowledgments

Many thanks to Nina Hess, Steve Winter,
Peter Archer, and Rob King

KNIGHTS
OF THE
SILVER
DRAGON

TM

A young thief.
A wizard's apprentice.
A twelve-year-old boy.
Meet the Knights of
the Silver Dragon!

SECRET OF THE SPIRITKEEPER
Matt Forbeck

Can Moyra, Kellach, and Driskoll unlock the secret of the
spiritkeeper in time to rescue their beloved wizard friend?

August 2004

RIDDLE IN STONE
Ree Soesbee

Will the Knights unravel the statue's riddle
before more people turn to stone?

August 2004

SIGN OF THE SHAPESHIFTER
Dale Donovan and Linda Johns

Can Kellach and Driskoll find the shapeshifter
before he ruins their father?

October 2004

EYE OF FORTUNE
Denise R. Graham

Does the fortuneteller's prophecy spell doom
for the Knights? Or unheard-of treasure?

December 2004

For ages 8 and up